Clash
of the
Figments

Blaine Staat

Linear Wave Media
P.O. Box 177
Liberty, KY 42539

Clash of the Figments

Chapter 1

I didn't poop my shorts until much later – and I'll never tell you exactly when I did – but it all started like this:

The last body falls to the ground and Tingaard the Mongol sheathes his sword. He marches across the battlefield, oblivious to the smoke and human carnage all around, making his way straight towards the shivering damsel. Wide-eyed with terror, she tries to push herself further into the corner. A whimper escapes her trembling lips.

Tingaard stops and stands like a giant in front of her. His arm reaches towards her with an open palm.

"Give me the delicious gum," he says.

I reread the page and pictured it again in my mind's eye. It was epic. It was bold. It was fraught with glory, conquest, and the spoils of war. It was also unbelievably stupid.

And, upon further reflection, probably too introspective and moody for a Chiclets commercial. I sighed, balled the paper in my hand, and launched another air ball at the steel wire wastebasket in the corner. 12 for 18. 66%. Not a free throw percentage to brag about but good enough to be a multi-million dollar center for any pro basketball team.

I'm not a writer by trade, but business was slow. In this town, business was always slow in my *real* line of work. This writing biz, not really my strong point. Just trying to earn a few Lincolns on the side. What puzzled me was that I was having such a hard time with it. Four hours and still at square one. I'd never tried to write a television commercial before, but, jeez, how hard could it be? Especially for a stupid box of gum.

Kicking my ass though.

I threaded another sheet of paper into the beat up Smith-Corona and stared at the field of white. Puzzled. Why should this be so hard? After all, I had a bachelor's degree in English Composition. Or was it Paleoanthropology? Maybe Medieval History. . . . . Hell, who could remember? That was nine years ago at least. Point was, I had a degree in *something*, and that in itself should be enough to belt out enough mindless crap to fill 30 seconds of air time.

I sat back and pondered the mindless crap angle. Could be something there. Then came the knock on the door.

I turned my head real slow like and stared at the door through the layer of smoke undulating across the room. It was just past noon but my office was dark; wood paneling, bookshelves, and those really cool vertical blinds with the wide slats all working together to keep the midday sun at bay. It wasn't just me either. Everybody thought they were cool. The blinds I mean.

The smoked glass window in the door bore a human shadow, the letters "RETISSAL DRAHCIR" stenciled over what would be its neck. I'll be damned. Could be a live one. And just in time. I leaned back, crossed my wing tipped feet on the desk, and called out.

"Enter."

I'm a dick, you see. By birth, by profession, and, yeah, sometimes by choice when needed. Richard Lassiter. Private Investigator. Run a little gumshoe enterprise here called *Top Dick Investigations*. And a damn good one too by my view, despite the fact that business wasn't just jumping through my door. That wasn't my fault. It's just that where P.I.'s are concerned – real hard-nosed, trench coat wearing, Stacey Keach looking motherfuckers like myself – location can kill you. And Orlando just didn't lend itself to the cold, overcast, drizzly grayness that my breed require.

Don't get me wrong. Plenty of crime in this town. What attracted me to it in the first place. I mean, we got enough wackos, sickos, and knife toten' street punks to make L.A. and New York look like a couple of blushing schoolgirls. And one might think that any town dwelling under the specter of a corporate mega-conglomerate whose entire existence centered around a giant rodent would invite enough evil and darkness to make a black fedora commonplace. But that just ain't the way it works in this town.

Little thing they got here called sunshine. Hot, bright, and, unfortunately for me, shitloads of it.

If I had any idea what was coming I wouldn't have complained, though. If I had any idea what was coming I would've shanghaied an airboat out of here and spent the rest of my days chasing down gators in the backwood glades.

Okay, maybe that's a little rich.

The door opened and, much like a fragged Messerschmitt, reality as I knew it took a screaming nose-dive. Mr. Jackson Burroughs walked into my office.

He was a Washington type, I could tell right away. Gray suit. Schoolboy glasses. Military hair. No doubt a messenger from one of the many acronyms they had up there in D.C. (And what better place for those institutions to reside other than a place that was in itself an acronym.)

"Mr. Lassiter." It wasn't a question. So either he had done his homework on me or he'd picked up on the fact that my name was pasted all over the office door in big black letters three inches high. Either way, not a man to take lightly.

I picked up the phone. No special reason. Then I put it back down. Made him look.

"My friends call me Dick."

"Okay, Dick then."

"You're not one of my friends. I was just letting you know."

He sighed, uncomfortable and impatient. Good. I like to stay in control of the situation. Especially in my own office. And always with an uninvited G-man.

"Mr. Lassiter, I'm Jackson Burroughs. CIA" Acronym identified. He held out his ID. To his surprise, I took it and gave it a closer examination. Never been impressed with a quick flash of a badge.

It was legit alright. Burroughs, Jackson Samuel. Fancy seal, real plastic laminate, important looking control number. I studied the picture. From the look of him I figured his ancestry probably had a long history of naming its children with the last names of famous dead guys. Probably had a brother named Johnson. Sister they'd labeled Coles. Homely looking thing, but with a rack of golden boheebos that could stretch a sweater so tight –

Jackson reclaimed his wallet with a quick snap and it disappeared inside his jacket. I motioned towards a chair and he sat down.

"What can I do for you, Mr. Burroughs? Don't get too many visitors around here. I don't recall having done anything recently to invite attention from the government."

"We've got a problem William. A big problem. That's why I'm here. We don't know of anyone else to turn to except you." Burroughs apparently wasn't big on small talk. But for that matter he wasn't too stellar on accuracy either.

"The name's Dick."

"Right, Bill. Sorry. I'm just a little nervous. Like I said, this is big."

I opened my mouth to correct him again on the name but then realized that it would be easier to just let it ride. Besides, what if he was right? I'd look pretty stupid then. So I just nodded and smiled back.

"Mr. Lassiter," he said. "We know about your past. We know you've been involved with some pretty sensitive cases. Lots of things that we in the Agency term 'Code Red' assignments. Top level secrecy and priority."

I had no idea what he was talking about so I decided the blank stare approach was the correct route to take. My silence seemed to impress him. He stood, walked to the window, and continued.

"I certainly don't expect you to discuss them, of course. But we thought that with your experience in these types of situations, coupled with the high percentage success rate that you achieved in dealing with them, you might be able to help us with a current problem that, to date, we have been unable to resolve."

Talkative little shit all of a sudden. He turned away from the window and stared directly at me.

"In short, we require your services in a matter of extreme national security," he said sternly. He turned away from the window and stared directly at me again. Damn, how'd he do that? Had to admit, it fucked me up a little.

He opened his briefcase, pulled out a manila folder, and tossed it on my desk.

"This is your assignment," he said, tossing the folder to me again.

I turned the package over in my hands and nodded my approval upon seeing the markings stamped on its rich Corinthian exterior: "Code Red Directives" and "Package contains 30% post-consumer content". What a fine, fine envelope it was.

"Well? Open it." This was Jackson talking again. A rather annoying habit that he seemed to have.

"What if I'm not interested?"

"Then we'll be forced to reveal your true involvement in that pesky little incident five years ago. You know, of course. The Cesium-131 debacle?"

I sat there, a deer in the headlights. No clue what this bozo was talking about. He must have figured he'd struck a nerve. He sat down, eyeing me expectantly. What the hell. I wasn't exactly booked up for the month, and I didn't really see a promising future in advertisements. I'd play his game.

"Ah. Of course," I said. I unwrapped the string closure and pulled out the documents inside. The top sheet was a picture of a moose wearing sunglasses. A lit cigarette hung from his lips.

"That's our problem," Jackson said. "Code name is Zodar. He's a rogue Soviet spy moose."

"Zodar the Spy Moose," I repeated. "Definitely a suspicious looking mammal. So what's the story on him?"

"He's a loose end left over from the cold war. Seems the Politburo dreamed him up in the mid 80's for deep cover work. When the USSR dissolved, he fell through the cracks and they lost control of him. Now he's gone bad."

Jackson was looking at me, apparently waiting for some sort of an intelligent response. He wasn't going to get one from me.

"Hmmmm." I said instead.

"You mean, why did they develop a spy moose in the first place? Good question. But think about it; who would suspect?"

I nodded. Pure genius.

"So what has this spy moose been doing since he broke ranks with the former USSR?" I asked.

"Corn."

"Beg your pardon?"

"Corn. And wheat. Barley and hops. Lentils sometimes."

"No shit," I said, searching my bag of clues and not finding any.

"You look confused," Jackson said. "You should be. The free world has never had a threat like this before." He paused for dramatic effect. "Zodar's a crop killer."

"A cop killer?"

"No, *crop* killer. More technically termed as

Agricultural Homicide. A progressive, systematic annihilation of the entire Fruit & Vegetable group."

"Wow."

"Wow is right. With his mighty antlers he's already leveled most of the commercial farms in Asia and Eastern Europe. At his present rate, he'll have completed his work there by the end of the year. After that, we believe he'll then move into Africa to wipe out *their* farming industry."

"That part won't take long."

"We expect a week or two, tops. And then, he'll move west into – "

"Iowa!" I said, my eyes opening wide with the realization. "This is serious."

"Even more than you think. Our intelligence abroad has brought another juicy tidbit of information to our attention as well. It seems the destruction of all fruits and vegetables has the nasty side effect of putting a real hurtin' on the Bread & Cereal group."

"My God. I never would've thought..."

"Who would?"

I had to admit that by this point I was getting quite frightened. Many of these grains were fairly important to certain types of beverages I enjoyed; namely alcoholic ones. But suddenly, just before I became a quivering mound of spineless flesh quaking in fear on the floor, a thought hit me¬

"Wait a minute Burroughs, I've got one question. Why don't we just replant the fields after Zodar has left?"

Jackson stared at me for a long second. "What are you trying to do, ruin the plot?"

"What? Well, no, but – "

"Then shut up. Trust me, this is a bad thing."

"Okay, okay, I'm sorry," I said, deciding it was time to change subjects. "So why 'Code Red'? If he's such a nuisance, why don't you just take him out?"

"I wish it were THAT EASY. YOU SEE, HE HAS SPECIAL ABILITIES."

"How so? And by the way Jackson, you're talking in all caps."

"SORRY ABOut that," he said, shifting back to lower case. "Like I said, it won't be that easy. Zodar was not so much *trained* as he was *created*. I'm not saying that he's like an android or a Six Million Dollar Moose – do you remember that show? The Six Million Dollar Man?"

I admitted I did.

"What a joke that was! No way would he have been that cheap! Hell, we couldn't make a bionic *sperm* with only six million dollars! I can't believe the public even bought that premise! What a ridiculous concept! I can't stop shouting!"

And with that we both burst into long and hearty laughter. I pulled out a beer bong and we chugged some O'Doul's and pretended we were Beavis and Butthead for a few minutes.

"At any rate," Jackson said, back to business, "We just don't know that much about his past. But that doesn't matter much anyway because the problem is the present. *Whatever* he is, Zodar has a big trump card that he often plays when he gets in a jam: He's a shape-shifter. He can assume any form, any identity. People, things, animals - anything at all."

"What about adverbs?"

"Well, not those I guess. But just about any noun you

can think of should be no problem for him at all. A perfect camouflage whenever he wants."

"That could make it tough."

"That's why I'm here. An ordinary hit team won't work. We can't even find him. We need your special skills on this."

"On the bright side," he continued, "he does have a couple of flaws. For one thing, his antlers always seem to be exposed, no matter what form he takes. Turn into a bus; antlers where the side mirrors should be. A cup of coffee; big old honkin' antlers hanging off the sides. You get the picture."

"Good to know. Might be useful."

I looked under the photo and saw a dossier on what we knew about the hoofed villain. There was not much: Educated in foreign languages, ballet, and skullduggery at the Central Moscow Community College. Four years of undergraduate KGB training in Siberia. Proficient in Judo, Karate, Kung Fu, Antler Fu. On assignment (classified -whereabouts unknown) from 1986 to 1992. Started getting paranoid and unpredictable during the collapse of communist Russia (job security suspected as most probable cause). Officially reported as having turned in 1993. Whereabouts unknown from 1993 until 2004 when a 150 acre wheat farm was found completely destroyed by what was then technically described as "some sort of big mammal".

That was it.

I stubbed out my cigarette, wondering exactly when I had lit it. Or when I had started smoking for that matter.

"So. What is it exactly that you want from me?"

"Find him."

"That's it? Just find him?"

"That's it. You locate him, we do the rest."

"The rest?"

"Don't you worry about that. You just find him."

I had to admit the little gray suited sleazebag had my attention. This wasn't an assignment, it was a piewalk. No, cakewalk, cakewalk, that's what it was.

"I don't work for free, even for Uncle Sam. And I don't work cheap, *especially* for Uncle Sam. This will cost you."

"Don't worry about that either. You pull this off and you'll be well taken care of. Just keep track of your receipts."

"No money up front?"

Jackson held out his hands. "Mr. Lassiter, please understand the sensitivity of the situation. Officially, I'm not even here. The Agency can have no traceable involvement in your actions. Should you run into trouble, a large sum of cash could be traced back to us. We can't have that. You understand, of course, that we would deny even knowing you if this becomes public. If you succeed, however, it all gets swept away and you become quite a wealthy man."

It was definitely a tempting offer. Aside from the fact that there was nothing in it for me except a vague promise of some future grant of an unspecified financial reward by a man I had never even met before, it was perhaps the opportunity of a lifetime.

I turned on my potter's wheel and starting making a bowl as I mulled it over. Nothing quite like wet clay in your hands, spinning round and round, to relax the brain. Soon I was fast asleep.

I was awakened with a rough shake. Jackson again. Damn him.

"So what do you think Lassiter?"

"What do I think? I think it's a bad idea to pull the wheels off of three Hot Wheels cars and stuff them up your nose so far that you have to go to the hospital to have them removed. I know that doesn't really apply to this case, but still . . . "

"The *assignment* Lassiter. Will you take the assignment? I have to bring an answer back to Rochester."

"Thought you guys were out of Langley."

"Dammit. How does everybody know that? Yes, yes, Langley."

I let him squirm for a few more seconds. Boy, did I have this situation under control or what?

"Alright. Deal. But I'm gonna need some help on this."

"Lassiter, I already told you, we can't – "

"No, no, no. I'm not asking you for anything. I just want you to know that I won't be doing this alone. I have my own people."

"Are they good?"

"Are they good? Are they *good*? Is that what you're asking me?"

"That was the question," Jackson replied.

I leaned back in my chair and crossed by hands behind my head. "Let's just say that they're . . . . . not average."

"Above average I assume."

"Yeah, you could assume that," I told him. I didn't tell him that he'd be wrong as hell, but sure, he could assume that.

"Well then. I'll leave you to your work. There's no time to waste." He rose and gathered his things. I kept a close eye on him to make sure he didn't try to gather some of mine. "I'll be in touch periodically to check your progress."

"Yeah, got it," I said. "Hey, just one more question, Jackson."

"What's that?"

"You said the moose had a *couple* of flaws. Besides the thing with the antlers, is there anything else I should know?"

Jackson Samuel Burroughs smiled as he walked out the door. "Yeah. He loves the ladies."

And that's when I knew I would get him.

Chapter 2

A good movie has a way of staying with you. It can alter the way you think. Change your life. One of my personal favorites is a mid-80's flick called *Kill Squad*.

In it, some guy gets into some kind of trouble. Can't remember what. But apparently he needs some of his old buddies to help him with whatever it was.

He goes out to round up his first buddy and as soon as he finds him some bad guys show up and they have this big Kung Fu fight and the two buddies beat up all of the bad guys.

Then they both go to get the second buddy and as soon as they get there, *more* bad guys show up and they have another big Kung Fu fight and beat up all of *those* bad guys.

The same thing happens as they go to get buddy number 3, and again when they get buddy number 4. Once they were all together, they went and found the rest of the bad guys, had one more great big Kung Fu fight, and beat up all of them.

Roll credits.

I had to admit, it kept me guessing the whole way through. The reason I mention this, other than to relive a great cinematic experience, is because now I needed help and had to assemble my buddies, and I figured that this would happen in very much the same way that it did in *Kill Squad*, except for the Kung Fu fighting and bad guys and the fact that I only had to get two buddies instead of four. Still, pretty similar.

I picked up the phone to call buddy number one: Jimmy. I didn't get an answer and figured that there could be several reasons for this. To sharpen my detective skills I analyzed the situation and pondered some of the possible reasons why Jimmy might not answer his phone. Detectives do this. Keeps us sharp. I jotted down a few of the more likely possibilities of why Jimmy wasn't answering:

- Jimmy was outside
- Jimmy was dead
- Jimmy thought he was dead and saw no point in answering
- Jimmy didn't have a phone and I had dialed a wrong number for someone else who wasn't home
- Jimmy was standing on his kitchen table and couldn't get to his phone because his floor was covered with slithering cobras
- My phone was a prop

Intriguing, all. But I didn't have time to ponder them, so I decided to pay Jimmy a call in person. I grabbed my coat and hat and walked out the door. Got halfway down the hall and then ran back to get my snare. Just in case I was right about the cobras.

Damn, this is a short chapter.

Chapter 3

Never liked the beach much. Not a good home for a trench coat. I hadn't seen Jimmy in a while but I knew he'd still be there. Never strayed too far from the water for any amount of time. Last I had seen him, he was living in a rented house in Daytona a couple of blocks back from the water. I worried about that because it meant that he had to cross the street to reach the surf. Nothing bad about Jimmy, but I've seen roadkill that had more common sense around traffic than him.

Jimmy and me went way back. Used to steal hubcaps together in high school. I grew up and went to college. Jimmy grew up and, well, kept stealing hubcaps. Probably would've wound up a career criminal were it not for a little thing called aluminum rims. Jimmy never could figure out how to steal those and as hubcaps phased out, so did Jimmy's career as a thief.

To pass time after that he started a rock band called *Smash the Infants*. You'd be pretty safe in assuming that you wouldn't hear many *STI* tunes on your average easy listening station. But they were harmless. Just kids who knew how to really annoy the hell out of everyone. The band broke up years ago and Jimmy never really did much after that. Except surf. And help me out from time to time.

I've never been able to put a finger on what made Jimmy tick. In fact, further explanation at this point would probably prove to be fruitless. Suffice to say that

Jimmy was a living example of the classic inner struggle of intellectual well-being pitted against the respondent bipolar delusions of psychotic terminal stress as physically manifested in *both* sub-linear quadrants of the upper cerebral cortex.

He was fluent in one language and had heard portions of at least three others, a couple of which he may have even been able to identify if given a hint and a few guesses. He rarely wore underwear, and when he did, it was always something unusual, often with a farm animal motif.

I pulled up to his house around 3 o'clock. What Jimmy would refer to as "noon-ish". The yard looked as if it hadn't been mown in weeks. A VW bus that had seen better days sat in the weeds, with two spare engines baking in the sun on the ground around it, both missing what appeared to be some crucial parts. Trash cans on the side of the house were empty, which meant that all of beer cans and pizza boxes were still inside.

No doubt. He still lived here.

I left my keys in the car and walked up to the porch. I never worried about car theft. Anyone who stole Dick Lassiter's wheels was in for a world of hurt. Besides, not a big market for 72' Impalas.

The front door was open so I let myself in. Jimmy was curled up on the couch, snoring softly. To look at him, you might figure that he was the kind of guy who often got lost in his own home and wound up peeing in the kitchen sink by mistake. To know him was to confirm that.

I took off my shoe and clocked him in the head with it. This was fairly standard procedure. Jimmy lifted his head and tried to raise himself to one elbow but lost his balance and slid over the side of the couch, all in one graceful movement. He landed on the floor with a gentle *thud.*

"Wha..?" he said, looking around the room dazed.

"Wake up Jimmy, I need you. Preferably with a pulse," I said.

Jimmy groped under the couch and found his sunglasses. After putting them on he surveyed the room again.

"Are you the pizza guy?" he said, looking in my general direction. "How much do I owe you?"

"Put a cork in it Jimmy. It's me. Dick."

Jimmy looked around the floor, presumably in an attempt to find a cork.

"Dick? Whoa, shit. Hey man! What's up? What are you doing here?"

Jimmy staggered to his feet and gave me what I presume is a cool surfer hug. Hugs between grown men should be illegal. Jimmy didn't have a problem with it though.

"Got some business. Need some backup. Thought you might be interested," I said.

"Yeah? Cool. Count me in, dude."

" I haven't even told you what it is."

"Well, you know . . . hey, whatever man. That's cool too."

Jimmy's life knew no warmth.

"Sit down, I'll get you a beer," I said.

Jimmy's kitchen would give Martha Stewart cardiac arrest. Keeping the floor conveniently covered with trash prevented the need to sweep. There was a urine soaked

TV in the sink instead of dirty dishes. Jimmy didn't have dishes. All eating and drinking was performed with the assistance of plastic, paper, and Styrofoam. Saved on Ajax.

The fridge held three cases of Schlitz and a phone book. Jimmy liked Schlitz because he thought it was imported. I grabbed two, waded back to the other room, and threw one at him. He caught it on a one hop. We popped tops and drank, Jimmy after waiting momentarily for the geyser of foam to subside to a slow trickle.

"So," he said. "How are the kids?"

"I don't have kids, Jimmy."

"Oh." Pause. "Wife?"

"Nope."

"Oh."

An uncomfortable silence closed in, so thick that for a moment we couldn't see each other.

"Um, how about those Bears, huh?" Jimmy asked hopefully.

"Jimmy, let's cut to the chase here, okay? I'm alive, you're alive, and I need your help on an assignment of global importance." Just to make sure I wasn't wrong I asked, "You are alive, aren't you?"

He checked for a pulse. "Yeah, dude."

"Okay, here's the deal . . ." I sat down on a foldable lawn chair and filled him in on my surprise visit from Mr. Jackson Burroughs that morning, paying particular care to go over all of the important parts at least twice. After half an hour I finished and leaned back. "So, what do you say? You in?"

"Let me see if I got this straight. All we gotta do is find this Burroughs character and let the KGB know where he is and we get some free cereal? Nothing else?"

"No Jimmy, we find the Moose."

"Moose? What moose?"

"Nevermind. Just grab some things for an extended trip and meet me out front."

"Okay, dude," Jimmy said. "You know, I'm ready for a change anyway. The surf around here just ain't what it used to be you know? Pacific's dead. Tell you the truth, I've been thinking about moving out to the East Coast for a while. Check out the surf there."

"Jimmy," I sighed, " this is Daytona Beach. Florida."

"What?"

"You've been living on the East Coast for six years."

"Whoa." Bless his heart. He looked so lost. "That would explain a lot."

Suddenly, the door burst open and four mean looking guys burst in. None wore shirts. All of them had that "badass" look about them. They stared at me and Jimmy menacingly.

"Friends of yours, Jimmy?"

"Nah, shoulder hoppers."

The room erupted in motion and we had a big Kung Fu fight right there in the living room. When we finished beating up the shirtless ones, I nodded to Jimmy and walked out the front door.

I leaned on the hood of my car and lit a cigarette while I waited for Jimmy to pack. I had an eerie sense of déjà vu, but I couldn't quite place my finger on why.

Chapter 4

In the car, cruising up I-95. Top down, sun shining. My trench coat was hot as hell. Me and Jimmy were heading North to pick up our third and final team member. The engine on the old Impala wasn't running in top form. That plus the three surfboards sticking out of the trunk playing parachute were keeping us well under the speed limit.

In addition to the surfboards, Jimmy's "things" consisted of spare ankle cords, a roll of sex wax, three bottles of Hawaiian Tropic (SPF-2), two pairs of cutoff jeans, a couple of T-shirts, his electric guitar and amp, and a Gameboy.

"Where we going, Dick?" He remembered my name. I was touched.

"Going to run up to Wilmington. Pick up Simon."

"Prestwick?"

"Yeah. He's going to be working with us."

"Does he know that?"

"Nope."

"Oh." Jimmy looked out at the passing trees. "He's not gonna like you volunteering him again."

"Don't worry about Simon. I'll talk him into it."

"Yeah, well. You know, Simon doesn't like me very much. Do we have to get him?"

"Yeah we do. And don't worry. Simon likes you just fine."

"No he don't. He calls me that number thing."

Jimmy was right. Simon didn't care for him much.

Simon was at one end of the educational spectrum while Jimmy was at the other. A dollar says you can guess who was at which end. 'That number thing' was Simon's way of poking fun at Jimmy. He sometimes called him 'Number 12'.

It started when we were eating at a Thai restaurant one night. Jimmy had said something stupid (big surprise there) and Simon told him that most of the food on the menu was more intelligent than he was. At this particular restaurant you ordered your meals by number. Jimmy had ordered number '12.'

"He probably forgot all about that. Besides," I said, trying cheer him up a little, "Wilmington's on the coast."

"Yeah? Okay. That's cool." He seemed a little better. "Yeah. Okay," he said again. Personal affirmation. "Can we go a little faster then?"

"We're topped out, Jimbo."

"Really? I thought this big old thing had a V-8."

"It does, but one of the "V's" isn't working real good at the moment."

"Oh." Jimmy the conversationalist. "That's okay, I like riding in cars. I'm pretty good at it."

"Yes you are, my friend."

"I like watching things too," he added.

"Lots of good things to watch while you ride in a car."

"Yeah."

We rode in silence for a while. Jimmy ate some Fritos and then dozed off. Gave me some time to think. Jimmy and Simon didn't get along too well but both were crucial to my plans. Okay, that's a lie. Simon was crucial. Jimmy just needed something to do. But he was also my friend.

Having him along would bring some balance to Simon's extremely intelligent but obnoxious personality. Jimmy would also be a good sounding board. And, if we ran into someone with a gun, he would reduce my odds of getting shot by another 17% than if I had only one partner.

Cold reality. But it was a cold world. Well, except in Florida anyway.

We crossed the South Carolina border and almost immediately passed what was undoubtedly the best deal on fireworks ever offered. Made me think of Simon. Nothing to do with fireworks. Just that Simon had been wearing a yellow shirt the last time I saw him. Bright yellow. Just like the fireworks sign.

Simon was a square peg. As I've said before, a very smart man. Went to school up North in one of those places covered with vines. Harvard, or Yale, or Pepsodent; can't remember which. Maybe all four.

Maybe I'll grow a goatee. Give me an edgy look.

Anyway, Simon was pretty level headed. He was an asshole, but that was something I could live with since he won the intelligence battle between me and Jimmy hands down. Had an IQ that I figured had to be way up there in the double digits.

I met Simon when I was working part time at a Dairy Queen a few years back. Investigation business hadn't been exactly brisk then either. I went into work one night and Simon was in the back kitchen staring at the water as it washed down the drain from the running tap. I asked him what he was doing and he said he was "studying the effects of erosion in order to develop a theory which may provide a possible alternative to carbon dating".

I told him that I meant what was he doing *here*; in the

back of the DQ. He didn't work there. Anyway, to make a long story short, we got to talking and before you know it we struck a bond. I also got fired for fucking off in the kitchen for three hours. The breaks, I guess.

Simon apologized about getting me fired but told me that if I ever got tired of being a private investigator I had a promising career just waiting for me in the personal petroleum distribution industry. It's good to know you have that kind of safety net.

Simon always wore shoes because he had a couple of extra toes. This was the only thing that he was really sensitive about and he tried hard to act like it wasn't a handicap. Because he wanted to be treated like any other person, I always did my best to respect his wishes, though in truth this did create problems on occasion; especially when we performed certain field operations (like sunbathing) which inevitable led to his being left to guard some cheap hotel room, often for days at a time.

Overall, Jimmy and I treated him just like one of the guys, and, aside from some good natured ribbing from time to time, made no mention of his abnormality (we did, however, occasionally laugh like hell about it when he wasn't around; we're sensitive that way).

Although he was a pain in the ass, Simon was helpful and we had worked well together in the past. I don't think he really liked detective work and I know it rankled him to play second fiddle to myself. But he'd always accepted when I needed him in the past. Partly because he was my friend. Partly because he knew I'd beat the shit out of him if he didn't.

Like I said, cold reality. Ain't had my ass kicked by a pen yet.

We hit Wilmington around 10 that night. Would've made it sooner but we stopped at South of the Border to buy some authentic Mexican souvenirs.

Hey, who can resist all those signs?

Chapter 5

I'd forgotten about Pricilla. She was Simon's wife. She opened the door when we knocked. She was from some rich family with old money. She had gone to the same schools as Simon. She really hated our guts.

"Hi Pricilla," I said, feigning pleasure at seeing her again. I noticed Pricilla didn't bother feigning back. So much for social protocol. "Simon home?"

"If I tell you he's not will you go away?"

"Nope. We'll just come inside and wait."

"What if he's in Europe?"

"We'll make ourselves comfortable."

She glared at me for a moment. "Yeah, you would, wouldn't you," she said. It wasn't a question. A look of disgusted resignation came over her. "Well, get inside then." She turned and walked away without waiting. I would've checked out her ass but she was, after all, Simon's old lady. Kind of gave me the willies.

Me and Jimmy entered the house and kicked the caked up snow off of our boots. Good thing all they had in the foyer was one of those Persian carpets. Maybe Simon wasn't doing so well financially if he couldn't afford an American made rug. I also found it odd that there would be snow in Wilmington this time of year. Or any time of year for that matter. I was about to ask Jimmy where the hell we had gotten boots from when Simon walked in.

"Hello Dick," he said. "Jimmy." Simon was a little

shorter than me. Sandy hair, hazel eyes. Shopped at the Gap. Starting to get a little pudge overlapping his belt I noticed. Not much, just a start.

"Good to see you Simon," I said.

"Hey dude," Jimmy said meekly.

"I figured you'd be coming to see me any time now," Simon said. "Come on into the study. Let's hear what you're into this time."

"Looking good yourself, Simon," Jimmy said. He had been rehearsing responses in the car for the last 15 minutes. Wasn't hitting his cues perfectly. Didn't matter, Simon was already out of the room.

We settled into the study and, once again, I related the story of my encounter with one Mr. Jackson Burroughs. I finished and sat back in my chair, satisfied that the impact of this particular assignment was weighing in heavily on Simon. He stared at me for a full five minutes. I sat still but ready, coiled to spring into action should another Kung Fu fight be necessary. Jimmy was apparently also thinking about the episode at his home earlier in the day. He dozed only fitfully.

"Okay. Wait, wait. Wait a minute," Simon said, holding his hands in the air. "Let's not go any further here."

"Why, what's the matter?" I asked.

"I'm not doing a damn thing until I see the script," he said.

"The what?"

"Script. I want to see the manuscript."

"Oh come on, Simon," I said. "Don't start up with this again. Would I be here if it wasn't good?"

Apparently I could have been. Simon didn't say a

word. Just held out his hand. Waiting.

"Ahhh, shit," I said. "You are such a pain in the ass." But I opened my briefcase and handed it over. "Why do you always have to make such a stink over everything?"

"Because I'm not officially under contract yet and I owe it to myself to check and see what this is all about. If you were smart you'd have done the same. Too late for you, but not for me."

With that, he sat back and started reading. I waited impatiently, tapping my fingers, tapping my foot, counting to one thousand out loud, just trying my best to be as annoying as possible. Jimmy was sleeping more soundly now. He had a line of drool running down his check.

"This is it?" Simon said as he finished. "This is all there is?"

"Yeah, that's it. What's the problem?" I said.

"What's the problem? What's the *problem*? There's only four chapters here and part of the fifth. Where's the rest?"

"There isn't any more yet."

"Nothing? Nothing at all? Not a rough draft, a chapter summary? Not even an outline?"

"This guy doesn't work like that. He – "

"Look, Dick, I know you mean well, and I'd like to help you, I really would. But I've got a wife and four kids to support now. I need better material than this."

"You don't have any kids, Simon."

"Okay, that part was a lie. But the rest is true. I've got loftier goals than this author will ever be able to push me to."

"Dammit, Simon. You've been in some of the

dumbest plots ever to hit paper. Don't try that shit with me."

"Exactly my point," he said, leaning in and pointing his finger at me. "I'm tired of playing bit parts in second rate adventure stories that only come out in paperback. I'm better than that. A *good* story. That's all I want. Is that asking for too much? I don't think so.

"I mean, I'm not expecting to be in a Faulkner or a Hemmingway or even a Michener – too late for that. But damn it, a Clancy shouldn't be that difficult.

"What the hell, I'm even willing to get my arms and legs hacked off to get into a Stephen King. I'm talented enough to do that. But oh no, here I am in yet another unprintable schmuckfest of literary crap. I mean, this story sucks. Spy Moose my ass." Simon shook his head and rubbed his temples as if in pain.

"Oh chill out," I said. "I've been in worse gigs than this. We can salvage it. We just need to make a few adjustments maybe, that's all."

"We *need* Heather Locklear is what we *need*," Jimmy said suddenly.

"Well that's not an option we have at the moment," I said.

"Heather Locklear?" Simon asked, "And what in the world would Heather Locklear do for us?"

"What, are you nuts?" Jimmy said, looking at Simon's big old pizza head in disbelief. "Heather's like...like Mrs. Goodwrench. She can fix anything. *Melrose Place? Wayne's World II? Spin City?* Any of this ring a bell? Have you been dead for the past decade?"

"Okay, okay, knock it off," I said. "Granted, Heather

would be a big plus, but we're running on a low budget so it's out of the question. Why don't we direct our thoughts to something that we can do, rather than wasting all day on pipe dreams, hmmm?"

"I guess you're right," Jimmy admitted.

"Agreed," said Simon.

"Now," I continued, "If we do change anything up to this point the first four chapters may have to be revised. I agree, the plot is suspect. But I don't think we can trust the author to do any major rewrites at this point and still have us making forward progress. He's obviously an amateur and his editing skills have to be considered as such. So we'll have to just accept what is already done and make the best of it from this point on."

"Why should we worry about his editing skills? Isn't that what a publishing house is for?" Jimmy asked.

"What publishing house? We're talking small press at best. Limited resources. Won't happen. Trust me." Simon informed us.

"So we do nothing? Nothing at all?" Jimmy asked.

" I really don't think we can," I said. "And we've all been introduced so there's no backing out now, Simon."

"Next time I see my agent I'm gonna shove a toaster up his ass," Simon said.

"Maybe not the best career move, but that's your choice," I replied. The rain continued to batter against the window panes, painting a gloomy mood that echoed our feelings about the current predicament.

"Look," I said finally, "we're all good actors. I think if we pool our talents – "

"What about him?" Simon said pointing at Jimmy. "*He's* a talented actor? He's so burned out you shake his head it sounds like a maraca, brain cells bouncing around in there."

Jimmy looked hurt. And a little defensive. "Hey, man, I've had good gigs before. I've been a cop, a homosexual dwarf, a pregnant cat, a schizophrenic superhero – "

"Does this author even know how to spell 'schizophrenic'?" Simon asked rhetorically.

We all looked to see.

"Yeah, I think he does," I said. "'Rhetorically' too."

"Still . . . I don't think Jimmy's strong enough to pull his weight," Simon continued. "What else have you done?"

"Well, I already told you my big roles," Jimmy said gloomily. "That's it basically. 'Cept for that wizard thing."

"What "wizard thing?"

"Oh, you probably never heard of it. Way back when I was starting out. Before I got into sniffing glue, I played a wizard in a little fantasy story. Big tall old guy named Gandalf."

Simon and I both sat in stunned silence. My jaw dropped down so far I got carpet burns.

"You were in a Tolkien?" Simon asked softly.

"Tolkien, yeah! *That's* the dude's name! Man, that's been keeping me up at night, you just don't know."

"I don't believe it. You were Gandalf. That's got me beat. Man, you were really good," I said.

"Yeah," Jimmy said. "I was pretty good, now that you mention it. That book was probably the highlight of my career. Wish I could remember what it was called."

"Book?" Simon exclaimed, "Man, you were in a *trilogy*! *Lord of the Rings* is still selling. It's a movie, a video game; it's all over the place!"

"Trilogy? You mean, like, three books? Whoa. I must have started sniffing glue sooner than I thought."

"What do you think about Viggo Mortensen as Aragorn?" I asked Simon.

"He's good," Simon replied.

"Yeah, I think so too. But I wasn't too sure about him at first."

"Me neither. But by the time Boromir got killed I had kind of warmed up to him"

"Yeah, me too. Boromir went down hard; three arrows. *Thick* arrows."

"They were some nasty looking arrows too."

"But then Aragorn whacked off that dude's head."

"Well deserved, if you ask me."

"Wmmrerglumdmflml", said Pricilla.

"Hey," I said, "Who tied up Pricilla and stuffed a gag in her mouth? For that matter, how long has she been here?"

"Oh, don't worry about her. She's got some weird habits," Simon said, looking back at Jimmy. "Damn. *Gandalf.* Damn!"

"So that's good right?" Jimmy said. "We can keep going with the story, right?"

"Ah, what the hell," Simon said. "Why not?"

"Yeah," Jimmy continued, "maybe this will turn into a cult thing too. Kind of a new *Lord of the Rings* for the 80's."

"We're a tad past the 80's Jimmy," I said.

"Really? Whoa. That would explain a lot."

"So, you in Simon?" I asked.

"Yeah, I'm in."

"Good. Now maybe we can start actually doing something," I said.

I leaned back in my chair and took a long pull from my cigarette. When the hell do I keep lighting these things? No matter. All was well now. Simon was in. Jimmy was in. Pricilla was laying on the floor, hardly struggling against her bonds anymore. Simon was right, she was a weird chick.

We were a sly team. And we were ready to roll. First thing in the morning the hunt was on. The silence in the room told me that we were all thinking the same thing.

"I'm hungry," Jimmy said. "You got any Little Debbies?"

Chapter 6

Morning came to the Prestwick house. I awoke temporarily insane, confused by my surroundings. Gradually, the Miami Vice color scheme of the bedroom, the smell of breakfast hot dogs on the stove, and Priscilla's singing from the kitchen reminded me of where I was. *Hell Bent for Leather*. Judas Priest. What she was singing. Metalheads, go figure.

I roused myself and shook vigorously. Got dressed and put on my shoulder holster. Good place for a gun. Mine was a big long barreled job, custom made. Looked very similar to a .357 until you noticed that it had a barrel big enough to hide a roll of quarters. The guy I bought it from had told me it was a guaranteed "one shot stop".

Slight understatement. It would blow the head off a rhino. Don't ask; just trust me on that.

The fire alarm started blaring. Breakfast was ready. I padded off to the kitchen.

Simon was on the back porch, looking at the Wall Street Journal. Somehow I had avoided ever reading that particular paper in my thirty-some-odd years. No reason I could see to break a good streak.

Jimmy was still sleeping on the couch. He talked a lot in his sleep. Apparently he was getting ready for a dreamy punch out. His fists were clenched. "Hey, man you're not a local," he said. Oh, the demons that surfers endured. The clock read a little after ten o'clock. Jimmy had a few more waves to catch before he would join us.

I went in the kitchen and loaded up a plate with some chow. Priscilla eyed me suspiciously, leaning against the counter, holding a cup of tea in front of her with both hands.

"Touch me and I'll scratch your eyes out," she said.

I didn't reply. Just filled a glass with some OJ and headed out to join Simon, safe in the knowledge that my vision wasn't in any immediate jeopardy.

"I didn't know your wife was Cajun," I said, taking a seat beside him.

"It's not blackened. It's burnt." His eyes never left the paper.

"Oh."

"I'm sorry about last night. Making such a big stink and all. It just gets frustrating, you know?"

"Yeah." I knew.

"It just gets to me sometimes. I mean, I don't have a problem being the figment of somebody's imagination, but it just bothers me sometimes to know that everything I say, everything I do, and everywhere I go is subject to the whims of somebody else. It's just so . . . *controlled*."

"Yeah." It was.

"I don't know. I guess I just thought it might be a little easier to stomach if I felt that what I was doing was really something important. Something great."

"Yeah." It would.

We sat in silence for a while, Simon reading his paper, me chipping away at my breakfast.

"But on the bright side," I said at last, "Nobody in a Jack London novel ever got to blow spit bubbles. And, if memory serves, there's not a Kung Fu fight in anything Shakespeare ever wrote."

"Good points. I know, I know, I've got nothing to be upset about. This is a good gig. Well, good enough. I think we can really work with this spy moose thing. Which reminds me, when are going to get moving?"

"Are we back in character now?" I asked.

"Hell yeah. C'mon, let's go get Number 12 and blow this Popsicle stand."

We pulled out of Simon's driveway just after noon. Beautiful day. Clear skies, light breeze, 85 degrees. Strange weather pattern over the last 12 hours but I wasn't complaining. Jimmy was awake but had decided to go surfing.

"So, where do we start?" Simon asked.

"Need to get some money. For expenses," I said. "Figured we'd go buy some cars."

Simon grimaced. "Ahhh, man. Do we have to? It's so embarrassing."

"No choice. I didn't get advance money," I said. "Don't worry though, it won't take too long. We'll be done before dinner."

I pulled into the nearest car dealership – Chevrolet - and went to work. First we traded in the Impala on a new Tahoe. Pocketed the $2,500 rebate money and hit the road again. Next stop was a Dodge dealer around the corner. Traded in the Tahoe on a new Intrepid and walked off with another $3,500 cash back. I always wanted cab forward technology and I had to admit I was impressed, at least for the five minutes that it took to reach the next car lot. This one sold Toyotas.

The whole thing was ridiculously easy, really. Buy, get rebate, trade in, buy another, get another rebate. The only hassle was dealing with the dealers. But they never gave us a hard time because we usually bought some of the more expensive cars, didn't balk at their initial asking price, and agreed to whatever interest rate they quoted. We just made sure there was a rebate. That was the trick.

By sundown we had hit every single dealership in Wilmington and surrounding areas. My last stop was back at the Chevy dealer that we had started with.

We were driving a high end Mercedes by this time. I traded it in for next to nothing and got the Impala back plus the balance of the trade for the Mercedes, an additional $23,000. They were so thrilled at getting a brand new Mercedes at half its list price and unloading the Impala at the same time I think they shit their pants. Simon and I barreled out of the lot with a cloud of smoke and a grand total of just over $275,000 in our pocket.

I always wondered why more people didn't do this. Just don't like cars the way I do I guess. The real beauty of the whole thing is that all of the dealerships wind up invoicing each other for the cars that were bought and traded in, each one charging the next in a chain reaction that ends up back at the beginning, forming a vicious payment circle. They'd be busy for weeks trying to figure out what the hell happened.

Okay, okay, I said it was easy, I didn't say it was legal.

We drove back down to the beach where we had dropped Jimmy off earlier. We saw the Beach Patrol and figured that's where we'd find our man. Jimmy was pretty mellow, but he usually got arrested at least once whenever he went surfing. A most territorial lad when it came to waves. Luckily, they hadn't cuffed him yet and Simon and I were able to assure the bike cops that we would keep Jimmy safely away from the general public.

Simon threw his board in the trunk and I helped Jimmy unravel himself from the tangle of fishing line wrapped around his body.

"Surfing the pier again?" I asked.

"Yeah, dude."

"Nasty gash here," I said, pulling a good size treble hook from his calf.

"Yeah, that one hurt. Dude started reeling it in right in front of me."

"You mean you saw it?"

"Yeah."

"And you ran right into it?"

"Yeah."

"Don't you think that's a little extreme?"

"Maybe. But it was a good wave. I couldn't just leave it."

"I worry about you Jimmy. I really do."

We went back to Simon's house to grab something to eat and pack up our things. Priscilla had done us the favor of not bothering to cook any dinner. I'm not being sarcastic. It really was nice of her. Simon headed to his room to pack while me and Jimmy threw our stuff back in the Impala. Then we headed off to the kitchen to make some dinner.

I made some PBJ's for me and Jimmy since he had hard time with recipes that included more than two ingredients. While I lathered up the bread, he took the time to find a tape measure to check the length of the cut on his calf. Jimmy had a thing about scar size and kept a detailed record of all damage done to his body. Several trees had so far given their lives for this documentation.

Priscilla came in and sat down at the table. Just for fun I gave her a smile and she shot back a look that made my lips bleed. Jimmy took no notice. Didn't realize the temperature in the room had dropped 10 degrees. But then again he was used to cool. I said earlier that Priscilla hated our guts. I guess to be more accurate, she hated mine. Jimmy didn't really bother her. Probably because he didn't complain about her cooking.

"Ow," she said, looking at Jimmy. "That's a big cut. Does it hurt?"

"Yeah. A little," Jimmy replied.

"What are you doing, measuring it?" she asked.

"Yeah. I keep track of how big my scars are. I measure all of the wounds I get."

"Huh. From the looks of things you must be pretty good at doing that by now," she said. "Just do me a favor and don't give the tape to your friend over there. I don't need him trying something juvenile like measuring my butt with it."

"Oh, he couldn't do that anyway," Jimmy said. "It's only a 10 foot tape."

He went back to measuring his cut, the picture of innocence. Priscilla looked at me in a non-smiling way.

"What?" I said.

"Not a sound," she said. "Not one peep."

I almost made it out of the kitchen before the giggles hit and I vaguely remember a heavy glass object impacting the wall behind my head as I ducked into the hall. By the time I got to the front door I was laughing so hard I blew snot all over my hand.

I decided it would be best to wait at the car until we were ready to leave.

Chapter 7

It was eight o'clock when we finally hit the road for the Queen City. I didn't figure we'd be there long, but it was a critical stop since we didn't have any leads to follow on this Zodar fella. Not that we'd really looked yet. Actually, I didn't really figure to pick up any leads there either, but I wanted a new Panther's jersey and my mom lived close by so if we wanted a home cooked meal or needed to do some laundry we could score on that count. And then of course, there was Stinky Pete.

There's a little bar just out of downtown that I've used before as a source of hard to get mission critical information. I've also used it as a source of cheap mission critical booze, so it had the advantage of dual purpose. The bartender there was an ex-Navy Seal. A big biker lookin' fella, Stinky Pete stood about six feet-four and weighed maybe 275 pounds soaking wet. Worked a second job as a jack stand at Jiffy Lube. Strange source of information, I know, but he was plugged into the seamy underworld of international espionage like a lava lamp.

"Okay, you got me into this thing, so where are we going to start?" Simon asked. Sounded like a question to me.

"Charlotte," I replied.

"Charlotte? Why there?" he asked. Another question. Simon was starting to be a nosy little bastard. I started thinking maybe our trio was one too many. Lots of country road ahead, plenty of places to dump a body. But maybe killing him would be overdoing it a little. I decided to fill him in instead. That's the kind of guy I am.

"There's a little bar just out of downtown that I've used before as a source of hard to get mission critical information. I've also used it as a source of cheap mission critical booze, so it has the advantage of dual purpose. The bartender there is an ex-Navy Seal.

A big biker lookin' fella, Stinky Pete stands about six feet-four and weighs maybe 275 pounds soaking wet. Works a second job as a jack stand at Jiffy Lube. Strange source of information, I know, but he's plugged into the seamy underworld of international espionage like a lava lamp."

"Okay," Simon said, "but do you really think he's gonna know anything about a spy moose?"

"If anybody knows, he will. And Simon? If you ask me another question I'll break three of your fingers."

"Okay, okay, don't get so bloody hostile."

"Hey, man," Jimmy piped up from the back, "why don't we put on some tunage? Help everybody relax. Here, I brought my 8-tracks." He passed a bright orange case up to Simon.

"The only thing more remarkable than you having an 8-track tape collection is that this car has an 8-track player," Simon said.

"Well, you know, you can't throw out, like, *classics* man," Jimmy replied.

Simon opened the case and I took a peek. Typical Jimmy: The Angry Samoans, Violent Femmes, Black Flag, and, of course, the Sex Pistols to name a few. No Neil Diamond though. Simon would be disappointed.

Jimmy saw Simon studying the titles with a confused

expression. "Didn't think I'd have a collection of musik like that, did you?" he said.

"That's 'music', with a 'c', and no, I must admit that most of this was beyond the realm of my Music Appreciation classes."

"Yeah, it's a royal collection alright. Here," he pointed, "I haven't heard that one in a while."

Simon reluctantly complied and soon we were cruising to the melodious sounds of the Meatmen, the gentle rhythm of *War of the Superbikes* wafting through the night air.

Jimmy relaxed in the center of the back seat, arms draped out to each side, nodding with the beat.

Simon looked as if he were fighting the calling of a large bowel movement.

I drove.

"Yeah, man," Jimmy said, "I remember one night when we were opening up for the FPV's, before STI got famous, -"

"The who?" Simon asked.

"Naw, not The Who man, the FPV's," Jimmy replied.

"What is an 'FPV'?"

"It's not a *what*, it's a *them*, dude," Jimmy explained. "You know, The Phantom Panty Vipers. They were out of El Lay I think, had this real freaky looking dude playing lead guitar. Wanted everyone to call him Duke 'cause he wore this big thick collar around his neck and thought he was a dog. We called him Johnny Forehead instead 'cause he had this forehead that just kinda kept going back, and back, and back, you know? Used to piss him off a lot –"

"'Phantom starts with a 'P', not an 'F'," Simon

informed us. "They should have been the 'PPV's', not the "FPV's'."

"Yeah, whatever man. I mean, nobody said we were like English majors or anything. We played tunes, man, you know? We were *musicians*."

"Another debatable point that probably wouldn't hold up to cross examination."

"What?"

"Some people might make the argument that you weren't musicians," Simon clarified.

"Like who?"

"Like anyone who ever heard you play."

Jimmy was silent for a moment. Luckily, being in the backseat, he was downwind from me, or I might have gagged under the smoke that was no doubt belching from his ears as the fragile gears in his cranium ground together in a desperate attempt to determine if he had or had not just been 'dissed'.

Apparently, he had.

"Oh yeah?" he said.

"Yes," Simon replied.

"Well . . .well . . . *you* are."

"What?"

"Yeah, uh-huh. Don't know what the fuck I'm talking about now, do ya? Wish you did though, don't you? Huh? Don't you?"

"What are you talking about?"

"See! See! It's killing you, ain't it?"

"Dick," Simon said to me, "what the hell is he talking about?"

I looked at Simon and puffed thoughtfully on my pipe for a few seconds, surprised that I was smoking one and wondering when it was exactly that I had bought it.

"*You* are," I said.

Jimmy started laughing so hard he threw up all over himself.

Simon retreated without another word to the far side of the car where the air temperature was now over 110 degrees.

I drove.

Chapter 8

The rest of the trip was uneventful and we arrived in Charlotte around Midnight. A low haze from the steel mills blanketed the city, giving the lights an eerie lime green hue. Hue is also a village in Vietnam, but I think the slopes pronounce it "way". Don't say I never taught you anything. Cars drove up and down Independence Avenue and we almost hit a stray dog that came out from behind the Super Wal-Mart. Yeah, the Queen City was just as I'd remembered it.

Everything was looking good and going as planned until we arrived at our destination, the Roadkill Pub & Deli. That's where we ran into problem #1. The whole essence of the problem, I mused, was that the Roadkill wasn't there.

At all.

As we sat idling in a parking place where one of the eight pool tables had once been, the ever perceptive Simon seemed to perk up on the fact that something was wrong.

"What's wrong?" he asked.

"The bar's not here," I replied. Never give them more information than you have to if you can make them beg for it instead.

"What do you mean, 'the bar's not here'?" Simon pressed.

"Like I said, it's gone."

"You didn't say 'it's gone', you said 'the bar's not here'," Jimmy chimed in.

"Shut up, Jimmy."

"Okay."

"The bar is gone," I continued. "Apparently an overabundance of surplus asphalt coupled with the need for convenient downtown parking overcame the public's desire for fine dining in a family atmosphere."

"And strippers," Jimmy added.

"And strippers," I echoed. A desolate sigh rang out from all three of us simultaneously as we stared into the heavens and thought of what might have been.

"Such a waste," I said. "So senseless."

"Well what the hell do we do now?" Simon asked. Just full of questions, this guy. "I thought this was your "big source" of information, your "wired in" contact that was going to set us off on the trail of this moose guy. What do we do now?"

"I don't know, Simone. I don't know."

"Don't even start calling me Simone again. You know I hate that."

"Sorry. I'm just a little shaken up about this. Annoying you takes my mind off of it."

"Well you need to get your mind back on it and think of something fast. Three white guys sitting in a parking lot in this neighborhood at three in the morning is asking for trouble."

"It's midnight Simon," I said. " Not 3 a.m."

"How do you know?"

"Says so at the beginning of this chapter."

"Alright, midnight then. In any case we might as well hang up a great big banner with flashing lights that says "ROB US"."

"Okay. Hey Jimmy, we still got that banner in the

trunk?"

"Yeah. I think so," he answered.

"Oh, stop it!" Simon said. It appeared that our playful jocularity was wearing thin. "What are we going to do?"

"Hey," Jimmy said, "how did you find this place anyway? mean, you know, in the first place?"

"Just dumb luck," I said. "A couple of years back I stopped in for a drink. Got to talking to the barkeep & realized I'd stumbled on to a wealth of untapped information."

"Well, why don't we just go to another bar?" Jimmy asked.

Simon threw up his hands in despair. "What a bunch of idiots! What are the odds of finding another bar with a bartender who also happens to be an ex-Navy Seal computer whiz who keeps up on the current status of international espionage?"

I threw up my hands in exasperation. "Do you have a better idea?"

Jimmy threw up. "I don't know about all that," he said, wiping his mouth on his shirtsleeve, "I just wanted a beer."

"Oh my God," Simon said, " I can't believe I let myself get talked into this. I want out."

"Out of the car?" I asked.

"No, out of this book!"

"Hey, hey, look, we went over all this earlier. You can't go anywhere now. That case is closed. Besides, I think Jimmy may be on to something."

"You've got to be kidding! The *odds*, Dick, the *odds*. It's simply implausible that we'll find another source of information in a run-down bar. It would be too much of a coincidence. No one would believe it. And no self-respecting author would insult the intelligence of his readers by implying as much. It's just too ridiculous!"

"Actually it's no more ridiculous than anything else that's happened so far. But that's not what I was agreeing with Jimmy on. I kind of liked his 'getting a beer' idea. And if we happen to run into a good bartender, all the better."

"I can't believe it. What am I doing with you two?" Simon fumed. " You don't know how to run an investigation."

"Like I said, you got any better ideas?"

"Actually, yes-" he started saying, but before he could get any further Jimmy threw an Army blanket over his head and we spent the next few minutes beating the crap out of him. Now, I know that sounds a little harsh. Maybe even a tad cruel. Possibly totally unwarranted. But . . . . . . okay, it was. Violence for the sake of violence, pure and simple. What's your point? Hey, somebody shot Bambi's mom for no reason too, so don't go non-linear on me & Jimmy just for throwing a blanket party and kicking the snot out of some uppity Ivy Leaguer who, BY-THE-WAY, had it coming.

Simon decided not to share his ideas with us after all.

We cranked up the Impala and went looking for a bar.

Chapter 9

The Barking Spider was typical of the much celebrated hole-in-the-wall dives that we were accustomed to. Located about three blocks down from where the Roadkill had been, it was more importantly blessed with an agreeable location. That is to say, it was the first dump we ran into.

A prestigious collection of Harley-Davidsons, El Caminos, and two beat-up Ford pickups that resembled mud plows graced the parking lot and told us we were dealing with the edge of society. Not the top edge mind you, but definitely an edge. No faux-Euro aerodynamic styled vehicles here; just basic, down home, tobacco chewing, Rebel flag flying, proud of my 8th grade education transportation.

Neon signs in the windows of the bar informed us that Pabst, Miller, and some unknown brand called 'udweiser' were spoken here. Frequently and in great quantities from the smell that greeted us as we walked in.

I sidled up to the bar as inconspicuously as a stranger in an outdated hat and trench coat could and took a stool. Beverly Hills 90210 and Baywatch victim followed. We sat there looking around and nodding like three dorks who knew they had no place being here. Judging from the looks from the local clientele, there was no argument.

A tall, bearded barkeep that made Richard Marcinko look like a Broadway faggot successfully ignored us from his spot on the corner of the bar. The guy had Navy Seal written all over him. Literally. Tattoos covered virtually every square inch of his biceps; a substantial amount of real estate that resembled Earl Campbell's thighs. I had always thought the great Oiler's running back had retired, but was now convinced that he sat leg-less in a wheelchair somewhere, this choirboy having pulled his legs out from their sockets and now wearing them as arms. Cover this guy with a shag carpet and you have Chewbacca on steroids.

Suffice to say he was a large man.

"Let me do the talking," I whispered to Simon and Jimmy. Jimmy nodded his head, either in agreement or as notification that he was about to take a nap. Simon, of course, ignored me and decided to take charge of the situation.

"Excuse me," he called out. "We'd like some service over here. Pronto, if you please."

I winced. Jimmy snored. The bartender eyed his magazine for a few more seconds and then turned his massive head slowly in our direction. Metal on metal, the bearings in his neck screamed.

Oh shit. Simon, you idiot. I concentrated on keeping my sphincter securely fastened. The room became as quiet as a Sprint commercial and several people who looked like they had just broken out of prison headed for the doors. This gave me a pleasant feeling not.

When he came over and leaned on the bar in front of us, I felt like that dude in Jurassic Park that got sniffed by the big T-rex. I continued struggling to maintain control of bodily functions.

"Well now, what do we have here. 'Couple of respectable gentlemen. And in a hurry by the sound of it." He looked us over for a moment, then said. "What *can* I do for you?"

If his words sounded like an offer of assistance, the tone indicated otherwise. Simon either pretended to be an idiot or genuinely was one.

"Need some drinks, Jeeves. A draft for my friend here," a thumb in my direction, "and a pillow for this one." Another thumb for Jimmy who by now had his trademark drool line running into a small pool on the bar.

I shook my head back and forth. Godzilla noticed.

"What's your problem?" he asked me. His voice had that low, gravelly, you boys got 30 seconds to live quality to it.

"No problem," I said quickly. "I just wanted to state for the record that I'm not his friend. Never seen him before, actually." I turned to Simon. "Who the hell are you, mister?"

"Please, Dick, don't indulge the hired help. Know your place and they'll know theirs."

I could envision my place soon to be in an abandoned refrigerator in a long forgotten landfill. Whether safely tucked away in it or dead, at present I felt confident enough in that future address to go ahead and forward my mail.

The bartender seemed unaffected by Simon's remark and if he hadn't been staring directly into my eyes I would have thought that our chances of survival had improved. The pits of hell, however, never looked so bleak. "That's right, Dick. I'm here to serve."

Gravel. Lots of gravel. The bottom of a rock quarry during a landslide.

He turned to Simon and stood up to his full height, making several low flying aircraft change course. "*Sir,* may I recommend the house specialty?”

"That sounds fine, thank you.” Simon turned his head slightly to me and whispered, “Proper breeding exudes power over even the most savage brutes. Notice how docile he is now? Really, Dick, you have to trust me in these things.”

Dr. Docile returned in a moment with a beer, a pillow, and the house specialty. The beer looked safe enough but of course could have been poisoned, and the pillow, while seeming innocent, could certainly be used to suffocate Jimmy. But any fears that I personally might have had were forgotten when I saw what was placed in front of Simon.

"A Barking Spider. On the rocks,” the bartender said. "House special.” He leaned in close to Simon until their noses almost touched. “Enjoy.”

Whatever a Barking Spider was, it was not pretty. I found myself feeling sympathy for the ice cubes; they looked in pain. For that matter, so did Simon.

"Perhaps I'm not as thirsty as I thought,” he said.

I leaned into Simon and did him the favor of a return whisper. “You know, Simon, if you don't drink it, the power shifts from the proper breeding back to the savage brute.” I gave him a second to dwell on that and then set the hook. “Face, Simon. It's all about saving face. Be a big boy. Show him who's the boss.”

A grim but resolute look set Simon's face. The sucker was going to drink it. He glanced up where Earl Campbell's crotch should have been and forced a smile.

"Cheerio,” he said, and kicked it back. He wiped his mouth on his sleeve. Set the glass on the bar. Straightened his back.

"Well, now. That wasn't so bad."

The bartender had a strange look on his face. I didn't recognize it at first because I never thought it would be there. But sure enough, he started to smile. Then he started to giggle. Then he started to flat out laugh his ass off.

"What's so funny?" Simon asked.

"I can't believe you actually did it," he said, wiping tears from his eyes. "I can't believe you really drank that."

"Why should that be so surprising?"

"Because you're such a wimp. You have no idea what that drink is going to do to you." He knocked his laughter down somewhat. "But I do. Hope you don't have to operate any heavy machinery in the next day or two." He broke out into a fresh gale of laughter. About a "7" on the Beaufort scale.

Jimmy, meanwhile, was observing everything with all the attention that you'd expect of someone who was dead asleep.

Finally, the bartender got himself under control. He seemed to be in a good mood, almost cheery. It's strange and moderately frightening to see a man large enough to pop your head off like a zit look at you with mirth in his eyes.

"Sorry about that boys," he said. "I don't get to enjoy myself that often. Been a while since I had the chance to get someone to drink one of those." He nodded to Simon. "Your boy here is in for a wallop." He picked up the glass, wiped down the bar, and then stuck out his hand to me. "I'm Rok Hard. I own the joint."

"Rok Hard?" Simon repeated, his head wobbling

slightly. "What kind of stupid name is that?"

"Simon, I'm sure Rok here didn't pick his own name," I said.

"Actually, I did," Rok said. "Fits me don't you think?"

"Rather smacks of sexual innuendo, I'd say," Simon said. He turned to me. Apparently forgot why. Turned back to Rok.

"And I suppose your wife's name would be something along the lines of 'Vixen'?" he asked, suddenly having a difficult time keeping his eyes from working independently of each other.

"Nah, her name's Areola," Rok answered.

"Ah, that would have been my second guess." And with that Simon fell off the stool.

"He'll be okay," Rok said to me. "Won't be worth much for a few days, but he'll be okay." He leaned back onto the bar in front of me. "Now, maybe you can tell me what you want here?"

The first thing that popped up in my head was a strawberry shake. No lie. I didn't have the balls to ask for one of course, but if I had I would have been justified since I really did have a hankering for one at the moment and he did just ask me after all.

However, my vast experiences with establishments such as this coupled with my will to live told me that an order for a cool and fruity strawberry shake would probably be interpreted as a request for some inbred genetically defective redhead hillbilly to come over and beat the crap out of me.

So instead of actually sticking my head up my ass and petitioning a death sentence, or worse, my very own

Barking Spider (or whatever other arachnid type potions that might lurk in the bowels of the recipe file), I decided to go straight up with the man. So I threw out the whole story to him; the D.C. suits, the renegade Russian farm animals – the whole nine yards, plus a couple of extra feet that, while completely fabricated and untrue, gave the story a little more pizazz.

When I finished, I stubbed out my cigarette in the ashtray – when the hell do I keep lighting these things? – and drained the rest of my beer. Old hindquarter arms, aka Rok, just stood there staring at me. I hoped that he was considering how to answer my request for information and not trying to decide how much of me he could stuff into a glove compartment. He finally reached up to his face and plucked out what was either a hair or a small fir tree from his nose.

"Come on in the back," he said to me, motioning with his big ole' Andre the Giant head. "Your friends ain't going nowhere." This was true. Jimmy's drool line now ended in a pool large enough to stock with bass. Simon was still laid out cold on the floor; a pedestrian speed bump.

I followed Rok into the backroom and felt as though I had stepped into another world. Instead of a dirty slaughterhouse filled with meathooks and chicken feathers as I was expecting, it was as sterile as a bank waiting room. Same muzak too. Shiny clean linoleum flooring fit enough for Officer's County on any ship covered the floor. Four high powered computers with big color monitors hummed in the corner around a set of desks, and a large status board showing the layout of the globe hung tacked to the wall, many countries an explosion of red colored pins. The computers certainly looked impressive, though I must admit that I feared them more than I understood them. As far as I was concerned, a hard drive referred to interstate travel in a Hyundai. ROM was something you mixed with Coke.

The room smelled of disinfectant and the air was cool. A backup diesel generator sat by itself, ready to start up should any loss of power occur.

"Wow," I said, but it came out "Holy Shit."

Rok smiled and winked at me. "Yeah, pretty impressive, ain't it? My own private war room. Have a seat." He motioned to a chair and we both sat.

"I was wondering when you'd show up," Rok continued," Stinky Pete said you would."

"You know Stinky Pete?" I asked.

"Knew. Yeah, I did. Stink and me went back a long way. Desert Storm, Grenada, Somalia, Vietnam, the Six-Day War – "

"You're Jewish?"

"What? Oh, no. Just looked like a good time. So we got circumcised, grabbed a couple cases of Coors, and hit the beach. Not real sure who we were fighting there, but we blew up a lot of shit."

"Oh."

"Listen, me and Stink were following this moose fella since he attacked that first farm in Germany."

"I thought it was in Spain," I said.

"Yeah, Spain, Germany, whatever. What's the difference? Can't understand a damn thing they say either place. A foreign country, okay?"

"Okay."

"This Zodar dude is one bad piece of business. Got

everyone scared. Brass don't know what to do about it. So me and Stinky started listening in, getting the hi-pri dope and keeping track of this guy. Figured we stay on top of the situation and hang tight until the suits come and ask us for help. Everything's going just like we planned and then last night Stinky disappeared and his place turns into a parking lot. Nobody knows nothing."

"Oh come on, someone tore down his whole bar, carted the rubble away, and paved the whole thing in a single day? That's just a bit fast don't you think?"

"Work was contracted by Disney."

"Oh. Well, I guess that makes sense. Also explains why you can't get any answers about it. Disney's tighter than an inner mob circle."

"Don't I know it. Anyway, I'm glad you finally showed up. I got some stuff that might help you nab this Zodar character."

"What about you? Aren't you still planning to go after him?'

"Well, you know, now with Stinky gone, someone's got to mind the bar."

It was refreshing to see where national security and the threat of global extinction of all animal life on the planet fit in to Rok's priority list.

"Hey, no grog without a grogmeister," I noted.

"Damn straight. I consider myself a pubic servant."

"You mean public servant."

"Nah, pubic. Kind of goes with the name, you know?"

I did.

"So, back to the moose. What kind of information do you have on him?"

"Not so fast, friend," Rok said. "I don't have much company back here now that Stinky's gone. Let's maybe you and me sing some Neil Diamond songs before we talk shop."

"Stinky's only been gone a day."

"Yeah," he said. "Still . . . "

I could see that Rok was in the mood for a duet and without much else going and a couple of beers in my gut I had to admit the prospect of a little two part harmony was inviting. Four hours and three six-packs later, we had successfully crucified several dozen top 40 favorites before going coma. The rest of the night was spent filling the room with the sonorous snores that sloppy drunks are known for.

And before you ask I'll let you know right now that just because we were sleeping in the same room doesn't mean that any fag stuff was going on. So don't even think about it.

Chapter 11

I heard a "ding" first and then a voice told me that the seatbelt sign was off, but it would be preferable if I remained seated unless I had something important to do. Not those exact words, but I get paid to read between the lines.

Not sensing any treaties between world powers needing immediate facilitating, I heeded the advice. Instead, I slowly opened my eyes and looked around. Rows of seated people. Small confined space. Steady vibration & mechanical noise in the background. My initial assessment – that I was on a bus – was quickly replaced when I looked out of the window and noticed a pronounced absence of asphalt anywhere in the near vicinity. Accompanying this in close proximity was a serious lack of any land, apparently hanging out wherever the asphalt was. There was, in fact, nothing but a lot of feet and the blue ocean below. And me without my swim fins.

The presence of a wing was the final piece of the puzzle. In case you're not used to detective work, let me spell it out for you: I was on an airplane.

Like I said, I get paid to do this.

Not a lot of difference between a bus and a plane. Sure, your survival rate is a little higher on a bus if the engine suddenly decides to quit, but overall, not too different. We were stretched out in first class, me on the aisle and Simon next to me fogging up the window. I decided Simon had milked out this hangover thing long enough and taped over his mouth and nostrils. It took almost three minutes before his brain registered that it had no oxygen supply and would be legally dead in another 60 seconds.

His eyes popped open. "Mggfleduh," he said.

"What?"

"Mggfleduh! Mggfleduh!"

"Look, Simon," I said. "If I want to talk gibberish I'll strike up a conversation with Jimmy."

He looked at me quizzically which I thought was a pretty funny way to look and told him so. At about the same time that I realized he couldn't breathe, he realized that his hands were not tied together behind his back and he reached up to rip the tape off his mouth.

We both breathed a sigh of relief. Him, because life giving oxygen was again pouring into his lungs. Me, because his silly Groucho Marx moustache was ripped off with the tape. I thought it was an improvement. Simon then screamed, either in agreement or pain.

Remembering my first aid training, I put a handy alcohol swab on his upper lip.

"Welcome back Simon."

"Yes, thank you. And a good morning to you as well." He removed the remaining strip of tape from his nose, pulling out a fair quantity of nose hair with it. Good tape.

"Looking a little green this afternoon," I said.

"Ohhh, my head. Where are we?" he asked.

Since I had already figured this one out, I shared the answer with him.

"I can *see* that we're on an airplane," he snapped, " but *why* are we on it, how did we *get* on it, and *where* are we going?"

See, this is the thing with Simon that pisses me off. I mean, if he was so sure that we were on a plane, then why did he ask in the first place? And you notice how he immediately throws in not one, but four – possibly three – more questions on top of it that he knows damn well I haven't had time to work out yet. Just goes to show you can't believe what they tell you about Ivy League schools.

I shoved a knuckle sandwich down his throat and the questions stopped real quick.

Though I hated to admit it, Simon had brought up some valid questions. I decided that I should probably address them. But first, I had to satisfy a more important question. Like, where was Jimmy?

Fortunately, with only a few surreptitious glances around the cabin (this is where a trench coat and fedora work wonders), I spotted him across the aisle two rows back.

For the next several minutes I got a little ticked off since the words "aisle" and "isle" sound alike, but are spelled differently and have completely different meanings. Not to mention that both of them have a silent "s" for crying out loud which is just about the stupidest damn thing since the entire plot of the James Bond movie *Moonraker*. No doubt some uppity Brit with nasty teeth had thought up both things. Probably Roger Moore. I mean, he never quite "got" Bond, so why should he know shit about spelling? Didn't hold a candle to Connery. And don't even start on that dickhead in *Her Majesty's Secret Service*. That was the lamest Bond movie ever. Not only does he have the gall to replace Connery, but he falls in love and gets married? Please. Bond get married? Why?

At least they knocked the chick off before the end of the movie.

But I digress.

I spotted Jimmy across the aisle two rows back. Dammit, I already said that and now I'm pissed off all over again. Have you ever seen a boy named "Kaisle" or "Kisle"? No, never, it's "*Kyle*", always *Kyle*. Silent "s" my ass. The English language is so fucked up.

I heaved a sigh of relief at finding Jimmy, though whether that was because he was with us or because he wasn't at large among the general public I couldn't tell and would rather not speculate on.

About this time I also noticed that I was a humming a song. It was either *Meet Me in St. Louis* or Metallica's *Enter Sandman,* both classics in their own right. Regardless, the humming was a trigger, and it all came back in a rush; Rok Hard, the Barking Spider, Stinky Pete's mysterious disappearance, and some damn fine two part harmony if I do say so myself.

Rok was going to provide me with some information on the Spy Moose. Something to do with a foreign country. He must have given me a lead or we wouldn't be on this plane, but I couldn't for the life of me remember what.

My mind was blank between my late night warbling with Rok and waking up on this airplane, and try as I might, I couldn't fill in the gap. It was almost as if an entire portion of my memory had been erased.

That's when I noticed Chapter 10 was missing.

"What do you mean Chapter 10 is missing?" exclaimed Simon when I informed him. "What the hell happened to it?"

"Two possibilities," I told him. "First, we must take into serious consideration the fact that it may have been removed by the Spy Moose to conceal vital information as to his whereabouts. Obviously, something important happened in Chapter 10 or he wouldn't have risked taking the whole thing."

"Is he capable of doing that?" asked Simon skeptically.

"I don't know," I replied, "but we have to assume that he may have powers that weren't included in his dossier."

"That's pronounced 'dos – ee – *ay*', Dick," said Simon, "not 'dos – ee – *er*'."

"Yeah, whatever."

"What's the other possibility?" he asked.

"Well, this is only an outside theory. And it's a little vague. But it may be that the author wrote the first nine chapters on an IBM compatible laptop that he was using from work. Then, when he left that job for another one and turned the laptop in, he continued writing on an iMac at his home which, as we all know, doesn't have a floppy drive to back up his work. Then, in a fit of anger, and in an effort to purge the iMac of all of the unnecessary files that their 16 year old son had downloaded from the internet, his wife deleted almost everything on the hard drive, including the aforementioned Chapter 10."

"You're right, that is a little fuzzy around the edges. A little far-fetched too, don't you think?" Simon asked.

"Yeah, I think. My money is on the moose."

That settled, we began to contemplate where we were

going and what we were going to do when we got there.

About that time Jimmy stood up and announced to the entire cabin that he owned a planet. Apparently the fact that no person, country, or entity had yet claimed any of the planets had just struck him. Or maybe it had struck him a few days ago and he had been secretly plotting since.

"You what?" I asked Jimmy.

"I want Saturn. I'm just letting everyone know now, so it's like, official and everything."

"Explain."

"Well, I was just thinking, you know? About how in the old days dudes like Columbus and Magellan and Socrates used to just land on these countries, you know? And they'd like, say, 'Hey all you dudes, this land is like, mine and shit'. So, I was thinking that, like, well, there's nothing left to claim, you know? Except, like, you know – *whoa dude* – who owns the planets? Like nobody, you know? So, I want Saturn."

Whoa dude, indeed. I was amazed. Not so much at the prospect of Jimmy wanting a planet as him stringing together over 50 words in one stretch.

"I see."

"Yeah, you know, I mean, I think it's fair and all. I mean, nobody's claimed it yet have they?"

I assured Jimmy that no one had. I looked over at Simon to see if he had any input. He said nothing, but I noticed that he continued to breathe my air.

"So. Cool. It's mine. So if anybody ever asks, you know, like, who owns Saturn, it's like, hey man, Jimmy does."

"Okay. But why Saturn?"

"It's just way cool, you know? I mean, like the rings? They're like, you know, 'Get back' dude."

Get back indeed. I assured Jimmy that we would register his claim with the Federation of Planets at the first opportunity. Just to make sure it was on record. Jimmy seemed satisfied, but as a precaution, stood up and went around getting signatures of witnesses to his proclamation.

"So, okay, you guys can have, like, the other planets," he explained to the other passengers. "Jupiter too. I just want Saturn."

He was received with a few smiles and not a few looks of utter bewilderment, but Jimmy didn't seem to notice. Instead, he slipped the passenger next to him – an attorney as it turned out, but is that really surprising when you think about how many of those little bastards there really are? – a smooth Abraham and had him start preparing the official paperwork for his claim.

Simon informed me that he had to pee and asked if I had noticed whether anyone had recently gone to the bathroom, because if I knew they were occupied, he would just wait until he saw someone come out rather than stand outside the door, which would be not only embarrassing to him (since people would be looking at him and obviously would know why he was standing there) but might also make whoever was in the bathroom feel pressured, which might cause them to freeze up and actually take longer to go –

I could feel a brain embolism coming on if I didn't get away from him.

"Listen, Simon, not that you're boring me to tears or anything, but I'm gonna have a look around this tank," I said getting up. "Something here doesn't feel quite right."

"You mean . . ."

"Yeah, Moose-Business. Antler hanky panky. Call it what you want, it ain't good."

"But how can you –"

"Hey, with the fucking questions already. Just a hunch, okay? I'm gonna do a little looking around."

And with that I pulled the brim of the fedora over my eyes like the little kids playing T-ball for the first time do. You know, pull it down all the way to your ears and just over your eyes so you have to tilt your head back to see. Makes you look like a geek, but the little geeky boy look has landed me some prime tail in the past. And if my hunch turned out to be nothing, maybe I could score with some chick back in coach. It's all about priorities and options.

Timothy Dalton was okay, I guess.

Chapter 12

I walked casually down the aisle of first class toward the aft end of the plane. That's the back. Not sure why they call it aft, but they do the same thing on boats too although you can also call it the stern, the top of which is the fantail. No stern or fantail on a plane, just forward and aft. So right now I was moving physically forward to the aft section. This made no sense to me at all. Even though I wasn't walking backwards, I couldn't be moving forward if I was headed aft.

I got confused, had a small aneurysm, and fainted dead away to the floor.

I woke up a while later, looking up at the ceiling. At least I think it was called the ceiling. I decided not to blow anymore brain cells and refused to go further down that path. Besides, something had caught my eye to reinforce my belief that a certain Zodar the Spy Moose had been on this plane. Namely one set of fresh moose prints running all along the roof of the compartment.

Looking at the spoor more closely, I realized that there were only prints of his hind feet, which meant that he'd been tip-toeing. And though I was no zoologist (and in fact had no idea what a zoologist was), I knew that anytime a renegade Russian Spy Moose has been tip-toeing on the ceiling of a passenger aircraft, he's been up to no good.

The footprints headed back. To the stern . . . .er, I mean, aft.

I got to my feet, approached the curtain separating

First Class from Coach, paused slightly to steel my nerve, and slipped quietly through.

The first thing that hit me was the stench. A nauseating aroma of death and decay permeated the air, and I recoiled because of it. The second thing to hit me was a fist with four large knuckles, which came without warning from the side and caught me square in the jaw. I recoiled from that as well, watching my hat fall to the floor and settle in a pool of urine. I turned to face the threat – if anybody's gonna be punching somebody it's gonna be me – but there was no one there. Through the gloom and murk I could see a man running down the aisle on the far side of the plane, huge floppy antler shaped ears bobbing a quick retreat into the bowels of the 7 – somethin' – 7.

What the hell?

I raised my hand to my face. Blood. Wiped my injured lip on my arm. I bent down to pick up my hat. Pee. Wiped it on a woman sitting in 24-C. With the bodily fluid cleanup complete, I continued my way further into the depths of the aircraft.

Around the second stewardess station the compartment had embraced an eerie twilight. Vines hung from the overhead and a thick mist rolled around my knees, obscuring the creatures who scurried below. Two children in rags sat in front of a broken television, warming their hands by the fire burning inside. The stripped remains of a sport SUV stood off to the side on blocks, chopped down to the serial numbers.

I never fly coach.

I stopped to let my eyes adjust and lit a cigarette. In this type of atmosphere, it was the perfect complement to the coat and hat. Very 30's retro. But I didn't have time to enjoy the moment or gloat in the envious stares I was getting for long. A stewardess – one with a dick – appeared out of nowhere and promptly spouted off some airline regulation about smoking being prohibited. I told him I was happy for him but apparently that wasn't what he wanted to hear. He wanted me to put it out.

Still smarting from the fact that I'd been sucker punched just minutes before and now totally annoyed that my moment was being interrupted, I wasn't in the mood to hear it. So I cleared his sinuses with a meaty haymaker and parked his regulation abiding ass on the carpet.

Just a word here, folks. If you ever come across a big guy in the dark wearing clothes that went out of fashion 60 years earlier, and this same individual is just standing there in a haze of smoke looking like he might like to punch someone, it's usually in your best interests not to provoke him. Unless you have a horrible toothache and can't find a dentist.

I caught a sudden movement out of the corner of my eye, but by the time I looked it was gone, whatever it was. Probably a squirrel. But it did lead my eye to an area just between rows 65 & 66 that didn't look quite right. I went over, yanked a few people from their seats, and knelt down for a better look.

Sure enough, there was a passage beaten through the underbrush. I looked for trail sign and spotted several. After a quick check of the spoor, I realized that something had recently passed this way. I also realized that I had just used the word "spoor" twice in the same chapter. Maybe I was turning into Wilbur Smith. But if you've never read a book by Wilbur Smith, you don't know what the fuck I'm talking about, do you?

Fucking idiot.

I wondered who or what had recently come through the trail; my floppy eared friend with a penchant for surprise attacks, perhaps? Maybe.

I pulled out my gun and felt the pilot adjust the flaps to compensate for the weight of it. Working slowly along the path, I went even deeper into the bowels of the aircraft, the gaping muzzle of my gun staring into the darkness with a black dead eye.

The going was slower now. The terrain grew rocky and pitted. Complex mangrove root systems tried to snare my legs and the dense brush & improperly stowed luggage made movement almost impossible. My progress got so slow at one point that even I got bored with the whole thing and dozed off for a while.

When I awoke I had to chase two kids out of the barrel of my gun. They had apparently crawled in there for shelter. And of course one of the little bastards had stuck gum in the rifling groove so I had to waste more precious time cleaning that out.

At last I came to the rear of the cabin where even the airline crew looked like something out of a John Carpenter movie. I stood there, puzzled, as there was not a sign of my quarry anywhere. Well, perhaps there was a sign of him, but if there was, I missed it since I wasn't sure what or who I was looking for in the first place.

Then I spied it. One of the bathroom doors was ajar. Without thinking (okay, that's a lie; I did think about it, but only briefly), I raised the mergers & acquisitions end of my gun and fired off six rapid shots into the small room, the *"BLAM! BLAM! BLAM! BLAM! BLAM!*

BLAM!" of the weapon obliterating all other noise. I looked over my shoulder to see if anyone noticed but saw no looks in my direction.

Peering through the gray smoke and shattered fiberglass of the lavatory, I looked to see if I had scored any hits, but other than the general carnage and the decapitated rhinoceros, nothing seemed amiss other than a few gaping holes in the fuselage and the strong smell of jet fuel in the air. I shut the door and hoped no one would notice the damage until after we landed.

Since the trail had gone cold, I decided to make tracks of my own back to the creature comforts of first class. But as I turned to head back, I collected the second cheap shot of the afternoon, only this was no love tap. I remember falling back slowly to the ground, watching the primates in the branches above swinging and chattering in slow motion.

Then the world turned black.

Chapter 13

When I finally came to, I got up and ran forward, suddenly feeling the need to escape from the oppressive gloom. Elbowing panhandlers out of my way, ignoring the come-ons from the working girls (except for one brief conversation with a cute little dish in row 53 wearing a mini-skirt to die for; I got her number and promised to call), and finally just kicking one guy straight in the nuts for no real reason, I reached the curtain and burst back into First Class.

The flight attendant thoughtfully whacked at the reaching hands of the coach passengers with a canoe paddle until they receded back to their domain, the anguished moans & shrieks fading away as they went.

Weary and sore, I plopped down in my seat with a sigh of relief and realized that I had been gone so long that Jimmy now had a notarized deed to his new property and was in the process of selling timeshares on the outer rings of Saturn. Then I saw Simon emerge from the lav, which only confirmed how long I had actually spent in coach.

Simon sat down and I called to Jimmy to put off selling mineral rights on his planet and join an impromptu meeting. After the obligatory *"Whazaaaaaaa's"* we got down to brass tacks.

"Alright", I began, "What have you two found out while I was gone?"

"If you drop your gum in the toilet up there, don't bother to try and reach your hand in to get it. It's a waste of time. Or so I've heard," Simon offered.

"Yeah dude, and if you look at the chick in 3B when she goes for her wine you get a pretty decent cleavage shot," added Jimmy.

I bit my tongue so hard my elbows bled. "Let me rephrase the question," I said. "Tell me what you have learned that specifically relates to our *mission*."

"I thought I just did," replied Simon.

"What mission?" said Jimmy.

I didn't bother replying. Instead I got up and walked to the cockpit. I needed information and I needed it now. Like, where the hell was this plane going? So, not bothering to knock, I pushed the cockpit door open and instantly came face to face with the business ends of no less than seven serious looking handguns held by all three of the very serious looking pilots.

"*Freeze asshole!*" they yelled seriously.

Figuring that this might be a bad time to rush up and hug them, I did as they suggested, and rather than asking who was holding the 7th gun (not to mention who was now flying the plane), I quickly excused myself.

"Uh . . . . . my bad. Sorry, sorry. Nothing to see here. Sorry. I'll be on my way now. You gents take care. Just leaving the cockpit. Backing up now. Sorry again for the intrusion. Bye now."

When I had backed out and shut the door, I took a few deep breaths and then went to the lavatory and changed my shorts. All cleaned up, I took a different tact and approached one of the flight attendants, throwing a question at her and leaving it hanging in the air as tactfully as the smoke from the joint she was smoking.

"Hey there, stewardess person," I said, "when do we

arrive at . . . . ."

"The airport?" She said in all her blondeness, hiding the doob behind her back and waving the smoke away. "About 20 minutes."

Damn. Snookered me.

"Yeah, 20 minutes. That's gonna be great, just great. Say, yeah, this airport, um, what is it called again?"

"That would be AIA," she said with a bounce.

Damn. Snookered again.

"Good," I said. "Real nice. Tell you what, let's do something crazy and go out on a limb here for a moment and assume that I don't know what those letters would stand for. If that were the case – and I know that's a real stretch – what would be your explanation to me as to what those letters represent?"

"Why, the first letter in each word of the airport's name, silly," she said giggling.

"Yeah, thanks, that's terrific information. You know, you've been just a fountain of knowledge here. I really appreciate all your time you whacked out reefer smoking heifer bitch."

I retook my seat and waited for the plane to land.

Chapter 14

"You mean he was on the plane the whole time?", Simon asked.

We were sitting inside a café in downtown Amsterdam. As it turned out, our flight had been to Paris, but was forced to land early due to an abnormally high rate of fuel consumption. That can happen when the plane has six thumb sized holes in the fuel tank.

Our beers glistened with condensation in the afternoon light, though the Dutchies called them 'lagers' for whatever the hell reason. No Schlitz, Black Label, or any other decent beer available, we had been forced to drink the local stuff. At least it was cold.

All around us was a bunch of Dutch looking shit. Windmills, wooden shoes, and the like. Dutch stuff on the walls, Dutch stuff on the floor. Bunch of Dutch looking buildings outside. Lots of Dutch looking people walking around saying "Uten, gleebin, globin, globin" and such. Couldn't understand a fucking word they were saying.

"Might've been", I replied. "Never got a good look."

"Come on, Dick", Simon said, "First you see hoof prints on the ceiling, then a shady looking figure with antlers running away from you after an outright attack. Zodar had obviously changed into human form. Then he ambushes you again in the rear galley – probably disguised as a monkey – and then disappears completely. It just makes sense."

Actually, I agreed with Simon this time. Well,

everything except the "it just makes sense" part. But there was no reason to let him know that, regardless of how plausible it sounded.

"Could have just been a guy in a moose hat. They're popular these days, you know," I said.

Simon scoffed at the idea. "Moose hat," he said. "Hmmmph."

I reached for my beer and saw that while Simon & I had been talking, Jimmy had been busy knocking back our drinks.

"Hey, Dutch person!" I yelled. "Need another round of lagers over here."

I receded into my own thoughts for a moment. Why would we have been on a plane that also happened to have the spy moose on it? Coincidence? Why had we been headed to Paris and what were we now doing in Amsterdam? Why did I feel like the author had never been to Amsterdam? And of course, what had happened to Chapter 10?

Oh, and also, if the spy moose *had* been on the plane, how did he disappear into thin air when we landed? And finally (I think), how could you possible know the answer to that last question when you have no idea what happened when we landed?

Yep. That was it.

"Why don't you tell them?" asked Jimmy, who had a bad habit of sometimes listening to other people's thoughts.

Okay, as long as you realize that I'm not doing it because Jimmy told me to, I'll fill you in on what went down at the airport since it does pertain to the story in a warm fuzzy sort of way.

The plane landed on time & without incident, except for being at the wrong airport and almost completely out of fuel. Jimmy, Simon, and I (notice the proper grammatical sequence of names) quickly got off the plane and setup a perimeter around it to make sure any spy mooses who happened to be on it (if any) would not be able to sneak by us.

We checked everything coming off of the plane; garbage, luggage, pets – everything. Then we went back on the plane & went over it with a fine toothed comb from top to bottom (except for the last 15 rows in coach which were a little too scary even for us to search). If there *had* been a moose on board, he had vanished into thin air.

Puzzled and depressed at having what may have been a golden opportunity slip through our fingers, we re-entered the airport and made our way down the concourse to baggage claim, making the assumption that since we had no idea how we had gotten on the flight in the first place, perhaps some luggage belonging to us had suffered a similar fate.

As we passed by the haggling fish merchants and their patrons, Jimmy posed a ridiculous question.

"Hey dudes, what if the moose dude just got off the plane, like, with all the other passengers? You know, 'cause we weren't watching *them*."

Ah, naiveté.

I was actually going to let Simon answer that one, but, techno-geek that he was, he had spied someone with a Palm Pilot iX and immediately cut over to discuss the finer features of the device and the future of something he referred to as "wireless technology". Whatever. If he didn't know that wireless technology went out in the early 1900's, I wasn't going to tell him.

"Jimmy," I explained, "we're dealing with a highly intelligent covert operator. Disembarking the plane with the rest of the passengers, while appearing on the surface to be a sensible thing to do, is not the kind of thing these animals do. It's way too obvious. No, mammals such as these avoid brightly lit public places. Too easy to be spotted and have their cover blown."

"Oh, I guess you're right," he said, stepping into a large pile of fresh steaming feces, "I just thought maybe he could have just disappeared into the crowd."

For a moment I felt a tingle in my neck as I considered what Jimmy had said. It sounded as though he had put together a coherent thought that actually had a plausible ring to it.

But as quickly as it had arrived, it left as I remembered who I was speaking to. Jimmy was, after all, a guy who had buried his flip-flops in his backyard when the strap on one of them broke and then mourned them for weeks afterward by refusing to wear anything but his black Tom Petty & The Heartbreakers *"Damn the Torpedoes"* tour shirt.

The waffling aroma of raw cod tickled my nostrils & prompted me to look over to a vendor a few feet away offering a ridiculously low price on the fabled undersea creatures. I could resist temptation no more.

"Hey Jimmy," I said, "clean the moose-poop off of your shoes and hang tight while I get us some lunch."

I sauntered over to the stand, which looked as if it had just been erected; somewhat hastily and in the last few minutes in fact. The proprietor had on one of those silly hats with the antlers. Told you they were popular, even if it wasn't until later in the day when we were drinking beer at that café. I selected a few of the 20-ouncers and paid the man.

"Nice hat," I said, walking away. He just stared at me with his large brown eyes and oversized snout.

Jimmy and I continued down the concourse, eating on the go since we felt it was in the best interests of a crucial mission to look as if you had no time to lose.

Just as we reached the baggage carousel, Simon showed back up with a woman on his arm. I won't say she was a dog – because I did that once and caught no end of shit from every feminist group east of Texas – but when she saw the extra fish we had bought for Simon, she raised up on her hind legs and begged.

"Hi guys, this is Susan. I love her. We're going to get married." Simon proclaimed.

"Simon, you're already married," I replied.

"Not in this country."

I handed him the fish. "We don't have time for this Simon. Lose the Schnauzer; we've got work to do."

"Okay," he said. Then, looking at Susan, "Hit the bricks Fido." He threw the fish across the concourse and Susan bounded after it.

We never saw her again.

As it turned out, Simon and I did have luggage on the carousel waiting for us. It was easy to tell the bags belonged to us since each had our names stenciled on them in 6" block white letters. Jimmy actually had no bag, but there was a surfboard with a pair of socks taped to it which we assumed was his.

We picked up our stuff along with a couple of other

suitcases that did not belong to us but probably could have.

Outside we hailed a taxi, which is unremarkable in itself except for a strange thing that happened as we were getting in: Some kid was standing on the sidewalk with his finger stuck in this big stone wall. Just standing there like a dork. As Jimmy was putting his surfboard in the cab, he happened to hit the little vagrant right in the crotch, causing him to fall to the ground doubled over in pain (the kid that is; Jimmy wasn't hurt at all).

So, as this kid is laying there, water starts shooting out of the wall from this hole that he had obviously made with his finger. know this wasn't my homeland, but I'll tell you, I hate vandalism anywhere, in any form, so I started reading this little delinquent the riot act right on the spot.

As I'm yelling at him, Jimmy noticed a ding on the end of his board that had hit the boy (although we now suspected nothing so innocent and wondered if in fact the boy had not thrown his balls at the surfboard in an attempt to damage it as well as the wall).

Jimmy doesn't like people messing with his stick, so he started kicking the kid for a while until he realized that he was wearing flip-flops and it was hurting his feet.

During all this, the little punk just keeps yelling about some dyke, over and over and over, but we didn't see any lesbians around anywhere so we weren't buying any of his excuses.

Figuring that we had taught the youngster a valuable lesson, we bundled into the cab, motioned the driver to move along, and soon felt right at home as we discovered that cabbies here didn't speak English either.

As we cruised down the streets, we gawked at the town, had a quick fart noise contest (Simon won; he's good), and generally enjoyed the ride. We eventually went down a street where a couple of drunks were puking at the curb; a sure sign of a pub.

And that's how we wound up here.

Chapter 15

Though it pains me to admit it, I was baffled by the events that had taken place so far, which was in itself puzzling. Compounding this was the ever growing despair that all of these things would make just as much sense – that is to say, none – when this whole mission was over, cleverly and maliciously avoiding the neat tie-in that would explain everything. Kind of like the movie *Eye of the Beholder*, where you watch it the whole time thinking that it's stupid and makes absolutely no sense but you stay with it till the end because you know that it has to be a good movie since Blockbuster had a whole section reserved for it and you're confident that if you just see it through something will happen to make it all come together and make sense and you'll say "Ahhhhhh! I get it!" but then it just ends and you wind up staring at the TV as the entire credits roll by thinking "What the hell was all that about?" and simultaneously being pissed that you just wasted $3.00 plus two hours of your non-refundable life and yet greatly relieved that you didn't blow $7.50 and the same amount of your life (plus gas for the car) and risk having someone you know see you coming out of a public theatre where the same credits happened to be rolling. And I'm in Europe so that is the correct spelling for "theater" over here so pack sand.

"Hay," slurred Jimmy.

"Thas 'Hey', not 'Hay' you shtupid . . . ," Simon corrected, kind of.

They were both seriously drunk. Jimmy was as

polluted as the Hudson river and Simon looked like a manatee that had recently been hit by a speeding Boston Whaler.

"I was thinking," Jimmy continued, "how many boxes of staples have you thrown away?"

"What?" I replied.

"Staples. Boxes of staples. Don't you think people wind up wasting them?"

"Jimmy, what are you talking about?"

"I'm talking about *staples*, dude. You know, staple, staple, staple. Where you click paper together."

"I *know* what staples are, I just have no idea what you're talking about."

"It's so simple," he said. "What I mean is that staples come in boxes of like, what? Five thousand, right?"

"Yes," I replied cautiously.

"Well, does anybody ever *use* all of the staples in a box? Heeelll no. You wind up loading your stapler one time and then you put the box in a drawer somewhere and you forget where it is. So then when you need some more staples you can't remember where you put them so you buy a whole new box – another *five thousand* – and go through the same thing all over again. And then before you know it, you've got, like, boxes and boxes of staples that you can never use in your whole life and nobody else can use them either 'cause they've all got boxes and boxes of staples too. So you wind up throwing them all away. I mean, what else are you gonna do with them, right?"

"Maybe build a steel Barbie fort?" Simon offered.

"I mean, if you *keep* them," Jimmy continued, "they'll just all wind up in the same drawer again since you won't need them right now and then when you do need them you'll have forgotten where they all were and buy *another* box. I'm telling you guys, it's a vicious cycle man."

"Jimmy," I said, "you're starting to frighten me. What the hell are you talking about?"

"Well, here's the deal. I'm thinking about this problem and how to fix it, right? And the only thing that I can think to do is to fix it myself. So I'm gonna start my own staple business."

"I thought you just said that the world is already overpopulated with staples as it is."

"No, no. I said there are *too many* staples. But that's because they make you buy them in boxes with *thousands* of staples in them, and *nobody* needs that many. That's how they get you."

"So?"

"*So*, with *my* business, you'd only buy the amount of staples that you *need*."

I felt like a kid in a grocery store who spent too long looking at the back of the Cap'n Crunch box and then suddenly looks around to find that his parents are nowhere in sight.

"They buy what they need," I echoed.

"Yeah, man! Isn't that an awesome idea? Like, say you're this dude and you need, maybe, I don't know, eight staples. Instead of buying a box of 5000 and throwing almost all of them away, 'cause you only need eight, right?"

"We got that part."

"Well, with my business, you could just place an order with me and I'd sell you – guess how many?"

"Uh, well, I'm going to think outside the box on this one and say, I don't know, maybe, eight?"

"Yeah! Exactly! Staples to order. You need eight staples, you buy eight staples. You need twelve staples, you buy twelve. You need – "

"We get it Jimmy."

"Yeah? Well, what do you think?"

"I think it bears more research into the marketplace," I said. "Focus groups, risk analysis – "

"I think it's the stupidest idea I've ever heard," said Simon.

"Oh yeah?" Jimmy said. "Well, what do you know?"

"What do *I* know? I'll tell you what. Why don't you make a list of what *you* know, and I'll make a list of what *I* know, and then well compare the length of *my* list with the length of *your* list and – "

"Alright, alright, shut up the both of you," I said. "Let's square up the tab and find a place to stay."

I called for the waiter and he placed the check on our table. We all looked at it but no one had a clue what it said. Taking into account that we probably only had 12 or 15 rounds, and the fact that the U.S. dollar was probably worth at least 20 times whatever they used for money here, we figured a cool five-spot would cover it and also provide a healthy tip.

We walked outside and surveyed the street from the sidewalk.

"So what do you figure a hotel would look like in this town?" Simon asked.

But before we had time to really look around, we heard a soft rumble in the distance which quickly turned into a loud roar in the near vicinity, and suddenly a massive wall of water came rushing down the street, sweeping away everything – including us – in its path.

"Surf's up!" Jimmy yelled and he caught the front of the wave from a standing start on the curb and immediately started shredding the lip. Simon and I cleverly clutched our bags in terror and just tried to stay afloat. We moved down the street quickly, bumping into cars, signs, and debris, coughing & sputtering in the salty water.

"Hey, there's a hotel," Simon pointed out as we drifted past a Holiday Inn.

Mile after mile we rode the torrent until we finally got dumped, bruised and dripping, onto a hillside in the outskirts of the city. Jimmy, of course, wasn't bruised or, for that matter, even wet. As Simon and I were recovering from our shock and dragging ourselves to higher ground, he zipped up to the embankment, turned a final 360, and stepped gracefully onto dry ground.

"Cool!" he shouted, obviously pleased by the impromptu inland surf and the lack of locals to fight off.

"What a weird country," I said, still coughing water from my lungs and dripping like a . . . a . . . a . . . uh, I don't know, a wet guy I guess.

At that moment a boat came through the water and sped over to us. Apparently a police boat if we were to pay any attention to the high pitched warble of the siren, the flashing red & blue lights, the big POLICIA sign, and the half dozen or so uniformed men on board all pointing guns at us.

A small boy – strangely familiar – stood on the bow pointing at us (he didn't have a gun) and yelling a lot of gibberish that we couldn't understand (big surprise).

We were soon transported to the boat with much aggression and a general lack of hospitality. Jimmy told them to quit it, but they didn't.

We were unceremoniously plopped down on a bench along the aft end of the boat (yup, just like aft on airplanes) with plastic zip ties securing our hands behind our backs.

The kid was still bouncing around excitedly and waving his finger in Jimmy's face and the cops were jabbering away at us too; probably reading us the Netherlands's equivalent of the Miranda warning and explaining what we had apparently done wrong. But of course we couldn't understand a fucking thing they were saying, so we just smiled, relaxed, and enjoyed the ride back into town.

We spent the night in jail.

Chapter 16

So the thing about Finnish jails is this:

You mean <u>Dutch</u> jails, Jimmy thoughtfully inserted.

Hey, get out of my head, you freak.

That guy. Sometimes, I swear . . . . Anyway, the thing about DUTCH jails – there, are you happy?

Yeah, dude. Thanks for the moment.

Don't push it surfer boy. So. Dutch jails are very unlike jails you find in America. Sure they have some things in common; steel bars, cots, criminals, etc. But other than the obvious, the similarity stops there. Foam pillows instead of feathers, a puny 19" TV (can you believe it? And black & white no less), only two HBO channels (no Showtime at all), and a remote control with only five buttons on it.

Like living in the stone ages. Or the 70's even.

To top it all off, they made us wear these ridiculous looking coveralls of the ugliest institutional green fabric *and* took away my gun. Foreign prisons had definitely digressed since I saw *Midnight Express*. I was all set to hit the law books in the library and work on my lawsuit until they told me they didn't allow that here either. Sheeesh.

We did, however, get to make a phone call each, but since no one really knew where we were (including us), or what we were doing (also including us), we were skeptical of getting any sort of positive outcome.

Simon called a pay phone that was located right next to the one he was calling from. Having nothing better to do, I answered it and we talked for a while until the guards got wise and told us to knock it off. At least that's what I think they said.

For my call, I dialed the hot little number from the airplane but got her machine. I left a message saying that I was in Rio finishing up the purchase of a new hotel chain and told her not to be a stranger.

Jimmy called his lawyer friend to get him started on a business license for his staple company. He was on the phone for an hour and a half, and I was rightly impressed with his burgeoning business acumen, but found out later that the actual conversation was only three minutes long; his lawyer had then transferred Jimmy to the multiplex theatre in Daytona where he listened to movie information for the rest of the time.

The remainder of our night there was fairly uneventful and quite boring except for the orange stuff that came with our dinner that none of us could guess what the hell it was. We still don't know.

The hours passed slowly and a normal progression of moods occurred as the minutes ticked by. First, the apprehension & fear of being incarcerated, slipping into boredom & impatience, and then, finally, into thoughtful personal reflection.

As usual, around 6:30 in the morning, Simon became convinced once again of his black ancestry, and after wailing "Swing Low Sweet Chariot" a couple of times started calling me "G-Money" and saying "word up" a lot.

As the sun came peeking over the horizon, Jimmy was still playing the air guitar in his sleep and I had come to the conclusion (after much deep thought) that Einstein was totally out to lunch on the Theory of Relativity because MC^2 actually = E, not the other way around. And I can prove it.

We were stirred from our reverie by a visitor.

"Yo, G", Simon called to me, "check out the homey." checked him out, but not because Shaft told me to.

The guy was obviously a local from the wooden shoes he was wearing, but I sensed an intelligence about him that I hadn't felt since entering this country.

"Good morning gentlemen," he said.

Thank God, somebody that speaks English.

"Whazaaaaaaaaaaaaaaa," replied Simon.

Showing unexpected good taste and breeding, the mysterious stranger ignored Simon. I looked for antlers, but found none.

"Richard Lassiter?" he asked, looking at me.

Since I'm a figuring kind of guy, I figured this was more of a pleasantry than a real question, so I told him I was indeed said Dick. He produced something from his pocket (thereby marking him as a producer, though whether an executive or an associate I couldn't tell) that I was very glad to see – a key – and unlocked the door.

"You're free to go," he said. "Your friends too."

With that he turned and started to walk away, but I wasn't going to let him go that easily.

"Hey, wait a minute," I called out, following him out of the cell area. "I need some answers."

He stopped. Turned. Looked at me. Damned near triggered a 'Nam flashback, which would have been especially weird since I had never been there, or anywhere else in Africa for that matter.

"Yes, I suppose you do."

We fell in step and walked out to the main counter.

The cop behind the desk was stacking our personal belongings so that we could inventory everything and sign that nothing had been taken. This was always a good time to make a stink about something being stolen so you could get free stuff on the taxpayer's dime.

Or so I've been told.

This one guy I know had scammed a cellphone, a subscription to Sports Illustrated, a new bike helmet, two puppies, a complete bedroom suite, and a gold ingot simply by throwing a snit at the police checkout counter. I could certainly have used a new watch but I didn't want to lose sight of the one guy in this entire country who had the courtesy to speak English.

The same guy who was currently headed out the front door.

I left Simon at the counter trying to explain why his duffel was filled with lacy purple bras & panties. As I bounded out the door, I yelled at him to remember to go back and wake up Jimmy. Kind of guy I am. Don't be impressed.

I caught up to my guy on the sidewalk, took him by the arm, and led him out to the parking lot. I did this partly so we could have some privacy and partly so I could punch his teeth down his throat if he gave me a hard time. You didn't want to do that kind of thing in front of the police station, but next to the police station was usually okay.

"So, what can I do for you?" my unknown Samaritan asked.

"Let's start with your name and play it from there," I replied.

"Very well. I'm Freeley," he said. "I.P. Freeley."

"Get out."

"You've heard of me?'

"Duh. Like for years. You're the guy who wrote *The Yellow River* when I was in the third grade, right?"

"The same."

"Small world."

"Yes, but I wouldn't want to paint it."

"Hmmm. I guess not. You're a deep thinker I.P."

"I try to be."

"What do you know about Einstein's Theory of Relativity?"

"Enough to know that he had it backwards."

I gave him a knowing half smile and nodded. This was a guy I could definitely relate too. Or barring that, tolerate for a few minutes.

"How about we get a drink?" I offered. "No fag stuff, just a cup of coffee."

"That would be good," he said.

We found a nearby sports bar and knocked back a couple of high protein energy bars & a pitcher of Jolt Cola.

"So tell me," I said, "What the hell was all of this about? One minute we're sitting in a bar having a couple of drinks and minding our own business, and the next minute we're doing hamster impressions. And not a single explanation as to why. Well, none that we could understand anyway. What gives?"

Old I.P. then talked at length, outlining the events leading up to our arrest and subsequent release. I faded in and out, only listening to about half of it – hey, I was up all night – but catching the pertinent portions. Nice guy, but he was boring me to tears.

The gist of it was this: they blamed us for effectively destroying the entire country by dis-enabling their flood control mechanism. First, I thought this to be a great overreaction. Okay, sure, we were knee deep in mud & debris, the roads & bridges had washed away, and 80% of the population was now homeless, but the country was still *there*. I mean, the borders might not be visible anymore, but I'm sure they hadn't shifted or anything.

And, P.S., I think that if the entire infrastructure of a country can be completely wiped out because some kid gets whacked in the nuts with a surfboard, it probably wasn't in the best of shape to begin with and excuse us if accidents happen.

We also underpaid our bar tab a wee bit, but I considered that to be entirely their fault.

The interesting thing – and I started to completely ignore I.P. once he mentioned it, even though he seemed pleased enough with his own conversation not to notice – was how & why we were released. Someone had paid our bail. Someone large and fuzzy with a strange hat.

Things were getting curiouser and curiouser.

Chapter 17

When I left Mr. Freeley he was still pontificating at length on some subject of apparent national importance but of no use to me. He was on his fourth V-8 and feeling it. I don't think he even noticed me leaving and I wasn't going to tell him.

I waded through the muck back to the police station to collect my bags and my partners. Briefly entertained the idea of not collecting either. Decided I'd be nice.

It bothered me that I still didn't know why we had come to this country. Other than experiencing the ambiance of the local drunk tank and the thrill of white water rafting sans raft, I hadn't learned anything and felt no closer to my quarry than before. If there were any clues to be found here, they were now buried under several feet of mud. I dig for clues, but not with a shovel, so if there was something to be found here other than a one-way ticket to someplace else, I didn't have the motivation to look.

Jimmy & Simon were entertaining the cops by doing their mime routine, and the uniforms were red faced & rolling on the floor as they watched Simon try to help Jimmy escape from an invisible box. I tolerate few things well and no things French, so this little pantomime came to an abrupt end as I pushed through the double doors. I glared across the room as my two Cirque du Soleil rejects put their imaginary tails between their legs and grabbed our things. I told the cops they were idiots and we walked out.

"That was pretty rude, Dick," Simon told me.

"Why? They *were* idiots," I said.

"No, not that. I meant interrupting our show."

"Yeah dude," Jimmy said sullenly, "They were getting into it. And we're good at it too, you know? I mean, just because you had a bad childhood experience with – "

"I said never to talk about that," I snapped. "Never."

"Sorry man. It just doesn't seem fair to us is all."

I looked at them both, two grown men standing there moping. Heads down, kicking aimlessly at the ground. Jeez.

"Hey guys," I said, "How about a Slurpee?"

As expected, they both immediately brightened and were soon chatting amiably with wide eyed anticipation as we headed down the street to the 7-Eleven. Jimmy and Simon each got a 34-ouncer, though they were different flavors.

Like you care.

I passed on the refreshment and picked up a newspaper instead, going stock still as I looked at the front page. I couldn't read it of course; foreign countries apparently never figure that they will have a visitor who doesn't know their local language. Not like in America where we pander to every race, culture, and ethnicity by providing more media for people too lazy to speak English than we do for those of us who took the damn time to learn it.

But I didn't have to speak the language in this case. Much to everyone's surprise – including my own – I had managed to stay conscious in high school geography long enough to recognize a map of the world when I saw one.

And my current experience with one certain international spy moose gave me enough insight to know what he looked like. Throw in my skilled deductive powers and it wasn't a great jump for me to figure out by looking at the picture on the front page that my mammalian villain (I like the way that sounds, don't you?) had just struck in Columbia. That's Columbia South America, not South Carolina.

Interesting that there's a Columbia in South America, South Carolina, and North America, but not North Carolina. Hmmmm. A puzzle to ponder another day.

Judging from the photos, mighty antlers and churning hooves had apparently laid waste to the entire agricultural industry of the country. Not really a big deal where foodstuffs are concerned, but the hit to coffee & cocaine had already resulted in a ripple effect of lowering SAT scores by 73 points and causing unemployment in the states to rocket up three percent due to layoffs in the DEA coupled with the mothballing of half the ships in the Coast Guard.

I whistled in appreciation of the mayhem caused by this one act and was suddenly slapped by some chick walking by who had apparently thought I had whistled at her. If she had looked half decent I probably would have let her get away with it, but she didn't so I slapped her back.

Then, of course, her boyfriend got mad and decided to do the honorable "man" thing and come to her defense so he punched me in the stomach. I've hit people for a hell of a lot less than that, so I did my best David Copperfield impression and turned him into a meat blanket on the sidewalk.

A few locals in the vicinity took offense at this and jumped in to try their luck. Jimmy & Simon then noticed the commotion and came back to the 3rd dimension long enough to jump into the fray too, and before you could say "Sprechen zie deutsch" there were people slapping and punching each other all over the place.

I was having a good time but feared a possible return to the local jail if the cops showed up, so I nodded at the boys and we slipped out of the bedlam and got a cab to the airport.

Chapter 18

"That has got to be the most worthless trip I've ever taken," Simon said. "I have to ask, Dick, what exactly was the point of that? We just took a round trip to Europe, and other than getting drunk and arrested, what did we accomplish?"

We were standing at the baggage claim back in Orlando International Airport. We had accomplished that much anyway. Tourists where everywhere; all excited about their vacations and getting ready to blow more money willingly than they could possible lose in Las Vegas under duress. Fine with me. Kept me from having to pay state income tax.

"If I had to guess -and I do since I have no idea -I'd say someone's trying to throw us off the trail," I replied.

"*What* trail?"

"The trail of . . . say, did you just ask me three questions in a row?" I asked.

"Um. . . no."

"Good, because you know what I . . . are you cranking me? You're cranking me aren't you?"

"What? No way, Dick. I'd never ask you three questions in a row. You know I respect you too much to try something like that. Besides . . . I don't want you to hit me."

Suddenly I noticed something that didn't look quite right.

"Hey Simon," I whispered. "Why did everything we just said have three dots in it?"

"What do you mean?" he asked, looking around suspiciously.

"Dots. Three dots. You know, I was talking and then ' . . .' happened. Then you started talking and ' . . .' happened again, right in the middle of what you were saying."

"Really? I didn't notice."

"Well *I* did. It happened on four consecutive exchanges. Something strange is going on around here. We were talking about three questions, and for no apparent reason three dots show up four times. This has got to mean something."

"Maybe just bad writing style?" Simon offered.

"Possibly, but I think not. No, no, this is . . .this is – "

"HOLY SHIT!" Simon yelled, "There they are again!"

" – a code," I finished.

"A code?"

"Yeah, an *area* code. 334. Langley, Virginia if I remember correctly," I said. "I think our CIA friend Mr. Jackson Burroughs is trying to contact us."

"But Dick, 334 isn't the area code for – "

"Just sit tight and keep a lookout for Jimmy," I said, "I need to find a phone."

Strangely enough, there was a phone nearby. In fact, there were a lot of phones nearby.

Almost as if planned, I thought.

I found an empty one and fumbled around my pocket looking for a quarter. Came out with a small white pill instead. I didn't recognize it and couldn't remember how it had gotten there, and for a moment I wondered if I was supposed to be taking some sort of prescription drugs, in which case it might be a really good idea to take it. But in the end, I just dropped it back in my pocket and lit a cigarette instead.

Sure enough, it took about two seconds for some yahoo airport employee to come bounding up.

"Excuse me, sir," he said.

I ignored him.

"Excuse me, sir?" he said again. "There's no smoking in the airport terminal. I'm going to have to ask you to put that out."

"Oh, come on," I said, "cut me a break. I'm looking all decked out here with the trench coat and the hat, and I've got a really important call to make. There should be some smoke here, you know? It just 'goes'.

"Besides," I continued, "if I went right outside these doors there, I'd be able to smoke, wouldn't I?"

"Well, yes, that's outside the terminal. It's perfectly okay to smoke there, but here *inside* the terminal there is a strict policy against it."

"Look," I said, pointing at the doors, "that's like, what, 20 feet away, right?"

"Well, yes, about that."

"I could walk right out there in five seconds, yes?"

He thought for a moment.

"Well, yes, but I don't – "

"What I'm trying to say is this: It's *so* close that if I wanted to, I could already be out there, could I not?"

"I don't – "

"Do you not agree that I could already be out there if I wanted to be?"

"Well, yes, but – "

"So by admitting the possibility that I *could already*

be out there, how do you know for sure that I'm not? And since we've already agreed that I *could* be out there if I wanted to – and let me tell you right now, I *want* to – the only reason I *wouldn't* be out there is if *you* didn't want me to be. Either way, I'm not doing anything wrong. So go away."

He started to say something but caught himself and slowly turned away, looking very confused. Good for him. If he had kept pestering me I'd have decked him.

"Hey," I called to him. "Spot me a quarter will you?"

He threw me one and I punched up 3-3-4.

A lady answered. "Information, can I help you?"

"Yeah," I said, "Jackson Burroughs, please."

"Can you spell the last name?" she asked.

I did. A few moments went by. I suddenly wondered if I had turned off my coffee pot at home and couldn't for the life of me remember.

"Sir, I don't have a listing for a Jackson Burroughs," she said.

"Of course you don't," I said, realizing that no one was just going to be dishing out phone numbers for spooks. How naive of me. "Just transfer me then."

"Transfer you to whom? I don't have a number for your party."

"Look, lady, I got a message to call the agency, and the only person there that would have wanted me to call is Jackson Burroughs, so please just connect me."

"Agency? Sir, this is information for Montgomery, Alabama. Are you sure you're calling the correct number?"

"Yes, I am sure. And you can cut the charade, alright? I know this is the CIA and you know this is the CIA so you can stop with the gatekeeper act and just transfer me."

"Sir, I can assure you that this is information for Montgo – "

"*Will you just transfer the damn call!*"

Pause.

"Hold please."

I holded. Er, held.

"Burroughs," said a man's voice.

"Jackson, Dick here. Got your message. What do you want?"

"What the hell took you so long?" he said, "I paged you hours ago."

"Had some trouble getting to a phone."

"Yeah? Why don't you get yourself a mobile?"

"Mobile . . . Alabama?" I guessed.

"*What?* No, no, a *phone*, a mobile *phone*, cell phone, whatever you want to call it. Where the hell did you get Mobile, Alabama?"

"Sorry. Something just fresh on my mind. Alabama. Sweet Home. You know how it is."

"I have no fucking idea how it is, nor do I care. Where the hell are you?"

I have to tell you, I wasn't especially pleased with the way he was talking to me. To be honest, between my recent conversations with Simon, the airport weenie, and the receptionist at Langley, it's really pretty amazing that no one had gone to the hospital by now.

All I knew was that I was now on strange conversation #4 and just about fed up to here on taking crap from people, especially someone like Jackson who was only being a macho dick because he knew he was a couple of the United States away and not in any immediate danger of being beaten and pummeled until he was black and blue and swollen.

"Earth," I said.

"Earth," he repeated "You think you could narrow it down any more than that?"

"I'm on land. That should cut it down by about 70%."

"That's as good as you can do?"

"That's as good as you're gonna get. And you got about two seconds to tell me what you want before I superimpose your face into a kiddie porn flick and post it on the internet."

"Alright, alright, calm down, calm down. It's been a little crazy here that's all."

"Yeah? You ever been to Amsterdam?"

"No, why?"

"Good times. You should go. Soon."

"I'll bear it in mind. Look, the reason I wanted you to call is because we're getting a lot of weird HUMINT lately. You know what HUMINT is, don't you?"

"I read Clancy. Human intelligence. Spy reports."

"Right, okay, well, the stuff we're getting in doesn't make any sense. Did you know that people all over the world are wearing moose hats? At first it was just a few sightings, but the damn things are popping up all over the place. Kids, grownups; all over the world. I'm telling you, it doesn't make any sense. Where the hell are they all coming from? Are they related to what Zodar is doing? We can't make heads or tails of it."

"Seen a couple myself," I admitted.

"Well that's just for starters, you won't believe the next thing. Get this: *Cod stands*. How does that grab you?

They're popping up all over too, just like hot dog vendors except they're selling *cod*. And people are going crazy for it."

"Not so strange. It's a delicious fish."

"You don't think so? Man, it just seems so *weird*. I remember being at Disneyworld one time and people were walking around eating turkey drumsticks. I thought *that* was weird, but now, hell, that seems pretty 'Father Knows Best' compared to cod."

"Okay. I'll buy in. Maybe a little strange. But what makes you think that's connected to Zodar?"

"Well, nothing really, except that I think mooses like to eat them."

"They do?"

"I think so," he said.

"Well, that would definitely connect the two."

Something was suddenly bothering me, a feeling tickling at the back of my brain. I giggled and told it to stop, which it did, but the feeling itself – that I was close to something – wouldn't go away.

"Anything else?" I asked.

"No, that's it, but hey, isn't that enough?"

"Yeah. Definitely some food for thought."

"Okay, I've got to go now, but stay in touch, alright Lassiter?"

"Yeah," I said, and hung up.

I walked back to the baggage carousel deep in thought. Stinky Pete, a trip to Europe, moose hats, cod vendors, and the missing Chapter 10. How did they all fit together? *Did* they fit together? That feeling in the back of my brain just wouldn't go away.

"There you are," Simon said. "I was afraid you forgot

about us."

The baggage carousel was deserted now except for Simon. Jimmy was making the slow trip around the island on the moving belt, still duct taped to his surfboard. I know that sounds mean, but he really doesn't mind flying as checked luggage and the money we saved allowed me and Simon to fly First Class. Okay, okay, we had more than enough cash to fly all three of us First Class, but Jimmy gets annoying sometimes too.

"Well," I said, looking at Simon, "why haven't you gotten him off of there yet?"

"He's heavy," Simon said, looking hurt.

"Oh, never mind," I said and grabbed Jimmy & his board and threw them over my shoulder. He was zonked out cold, cutting some heavy z's, so I didn't feel the need to untape him.

I grabbed my bag with my other hand, Simon grabbed his, and we went out to the parking garage.

"Uh, Dick?" Simon asked. "Where's the Impala?"

Chapter 19

Wherever the Impala was, it wasn't here. I figured that it was either A) still parked in front of the Barking Spider, or B) at whatever airport we had flown out of, or C) someplace else. Shouldn't be too hard to track down unless it was at "B" or "C". But that didn't help me now. We needed some wheels.

Simon could actually help in this respect, which is one reason why I bring him along on these things. He doesn't know anything *important* about cars – like which ones are cool, which ones are chick bait, etc., – but he does know some of the useful boring things; like how ignition systems work. That knowledge comes in pretty handy when you need to do things like hot-wiring.

He also knew how to open locked doors, but hell, I can do that. Only difference is that he picks the lock while I just throw a brick through the window. Sure, my way gets glass all over the seats, but it's a lot faster. Since he was along though, I figured I'd let him do it his way. It'd give him a sense of worth and none of us would ruin our pants.

"How about that one?" I said, pointing to an older (but cherry) Corvette. "I've always wanted a '68. Chrome bumpers, Candy Apple Red, and just look at that rear end. Bet we can score some real skank with that."

Simon sucked his teeth in an exasperated way, which meant that he was getting ready to correct me on something. This usually pisses me off and I've been known to pop him one in the jaw when he did it, but with my hands full with Jimmy and my bag, he probably figured he was safe.

"It's not a '68, Dick, it's a 1970," he said.

"Yeah?"

"Yeah. The differences are ridiculously easy to spot."

"Really."

"Yes, really. I could maybe understand someone not noticing the squared exhaust ports or front parking lights, but you'd have to be *blind* not to see the egg-crate side vents or wheel flares behind all four tires. None of which were available in either '68 or '69."

"Do tell."

"And GM has *never* offered Candy Apple Red as a stock color option for Corvettes – certainly not for the C3's anyway. This would be Monza Red, unless it's been repainted. And judging from the big block hood, this particular car has the optional 390 horse 454 with a 4-speed transmission and 10.25:1 compression ratio."

"Well. Alright," I said. "Is that good?"

"Depends on your definition of 'good'. If it's to go really, really fast and burn a shitload of hi-octane gasoline, then yes, it's good."

"Coolness," I said nodding. "Let's go then."

"Uh, Dick," Simon said, "There are three of us, and one of us happens to be taped to a surfboard. How do you expect us to all fit in this car?"

Just like Simon to ruin everything with realism.

I debated for a moment about just how much I really needed Jimmy along, but in the end, decided I couldn't leave him. He'd never figure out how to get out of the parking garage.

"Alright, well, let's find something else then," I said,

none too happy at having to pass up the 'vette.

In the end, we narrowed it down to two potential vehicles; a Plymouth Voyager (Simon's choice) or one of those new turbo Porsche SUV's (my choice). Simon droned on endlessly about all of the logical merits of the minivan; plenty of room for all of us and our stuff, built-in cup holders and child safety seat, blah, blah, blah.

I countered with the logical merits of the 450 HP Porsche, like having plenty of room for all of us and our stuff, scoring chicks, and having the ability to go 160 mph up a steep mountain path, should that ever be necessary.

In the end, I got tired of arguing with him and just settled it by throwing a brick through the window of the Porsche.

Simon wasn't happy about it, but he set about sweeping the shattered glass off of the seat and getting the thing started anyway.

I shoehorned Jimmy into the back and placated Simon by telling him that we were doing the right thing. Whoever owned the minivan probably had a lot of kids and a single income; taking their van would be devastating. Not having any children or a single income himself, this seemed to really strike home with Simon.

As for the owner of the Porsche, well, come on, it's a Porsche.

The handling of our newly acquired off road vehicle was a little squirrelly and took me a while to get used to. On the way down the spiral exit ramp, the rear end got away from me and I left some paint on the wall. Then, after paying our parking fee, I shot off the line too fast and grazed the barrier arm at the ticket booth before it got all the way up. Good thing it wasn't my car or I would have been pissed.

After misreading the traffic signs and circling the airport three times, I decided to take matters into my own hands and just drive over the medians and embankments in the general direction I wanted to go. I'll say this: although I sincerely doubt that any other Porsche SUV will ever have its tires actually touch dirt, they can rip up some sod if you need them too.

We headed up to Winter Land. Where I live. At least I think that's where I live. Hard to tell sometimes. Everything down here is called Winter *Something*. Winter Springs, Winter Haven, Winter Park, Winter Etc. Drove me crazy. On more than one occasion I wound up sleeping in someone else's house simply out of confusion.

Never caused a problem though. People were pretty used to that kind of thing. It happened a lot.

I figured we'd crash at my house for a few hours and sort things out. Jimmy woke up on the way and had to pee, so we stopped off at a Mobil station, stripped the duct tape off him (there was some screaming involved here), and pointed him to the bathroom. We picked up some chips and beer while we were there too.

The frenetic pace of the past few days was starting to catch up with me and I was dragging hard when we finally turned onto my street. I'm a man of action as you are well aware, but even us worldly types get fazed sometimes, and I'll admit that I was really looking forward to just being home for a while.

As I pulled up to my driveway, two things happened simultaneously; I suddenly remembered that I had indeed forgotten to turn off the coffee pot before I left, and I noticed a big smoking hole in the ground where my house used to be.

"Duuuuuuude, bummer," Jimmy said.

I sighed and felt my head loll forward as a feeling of utter dismay robbed my body of energy. I rarely do that – head lolling that is – but there are times when it is certainly understandable if not totally appropriate and I figured this was one of those times. Or the other.

Simon made an admirable attempt at legitimate consolation. "I'm truly sorry," he said. "What a rotten time to have your house burn down."

Idiot. Like there's ever a good time to have your house burn down. But that wasn't really what was wearing on me at the moment. Up until about 60 seconds ago, I wasn't even aware that I *had* a house, so I didn't feel a lot of loss. *That's* what was wearing on me.

See, that's the part about being a figment of someone's imagination that's the hardest to deal with. I find out about things the same time you do. I mean, let me ask you a question: what do you *really* know about me? Only what I've told you, right? You just automatically assume that what I've told you is only a small portion of my life. That there's a whole lifetime of experiences that you *don't* know about.

Problem is, there's not. What I've told you about me is also all I know about me. My entire existence, all the things I do, all the people I know -my entire world – is all subject to the whims of someone else. They want to burn down my house – poof – it's toast. They want me to punch someone – smack – I deck 'em, *even if I didn't really want to*. And I have no past at all. At least, not until someone makes it up for me.

Don't believe me? Okay, watch this. My house for instance, the same one that had apparently just changed itself back into isolated components of the periodic table, had been really cool. From the outside, it was nothing special; just a single story ranch. But inside it had a definite masculine feel; lots of wood, an open kitchen with a bar, and a sunken den with a 42" plasma TV and surround sound. Comfortable furniture. Nice covered porch off the back with a built in grill, pool and hot tub.

Now, all that? Everything I just told you? *It's bullshit.* I don't mean that it's not true – it is, *now*, and from the sound of it I'm really gonna miss the old place – but until *just* now, it didn't exist. I didn't know about any of those things until just this very moment. That's my life. That's how it works. I become aware of my world as it happens. And if someone hadn't thought me up and taken the time to write this, *I wouldn't be here at all.*

For a tough guy, that's kind of a fragile existence.

I opened the glove compartment and after rummaging around for a few seconds uncovered a bottle of Xanax. Didn't think the owner would mind my borrowing a few (at least not any more than he would at borrowing his car) so I popped a couple.

I sat back, evaluated the situation, and listened to Jimmy and Simon arguing over whether or not you'd die if you ate the stuff that was inside a Stretch Armstrong – Jimmy insisted you would – and started feeling better as the drugs kicked in.

By the way, I'm sorry for laying all that on you. Everybody's got their own problems and last I checked you weren't Dr. Phil. Hey, you either learn to overcome your obstacles or you learn to live with them, right?

Besides, it could be worse. I mean, I may only be a figment of someone's imagination, but at least someone *did* think of me.

"It won't kill you," I told Jimmy. "Do you really think anyone would be stupid enough to fill the inside of a children's toy – one with a fairly delicate rubber covering I might add – with a toxic substance?"

"I told you! I told you!" Simon yelled, smug and triumphant.

"Oh, knock it off Simon," I said. "We've got things to do."

"Like what?" he replied.

"Like finding a place to crash for the night."

"Well, we could get a hotel," Simon offered.

"Hey, I know what," said Jimmy. "Hold on."

He opened the door, scrambled over to my mailbox, and after heaving and pulling for a few minutes was able to get it out of the ground. He ran with it down the street to the house next door, the one that belonged to the Mitchell's, who were visiting relatives in Virginia. He struggled with their mailbox for a few minutes, and after finally yanking it up, stuck mine in the ground in its place, then put the Mitchell's mailbox back where mine used to be. The switch complete, he jumped back into the car, grinning like a kid.

"Check it out man," he said.

"Oh, that's just *stupid*," Simon said. "I mean, what? We're already driving a stolen car, now were just going to move in next door, pretend that this is Dick's house and that it was actually his neighbor's house that burned down?"

"Hold on there, Simon," I said. "This might work out

just fine. I mean, I've always liked Bob & Janey's house, and let's face it, I've owned hammers that were smarter than they are. They might not notice."

Simon didn't like it, but hey, big surprise there. We parked the car and got our stuff out. I checked out my new digs, noticed that my yard looked a little shaggy, and made a mental note to fire my lawn service. It only takes one bad neighbor to ruin a good neighborhood.

I have to admit, it felt right, my new house. And when my old key unlocked the door, I knew that it was meant to be. Either that or I've been having an affair with Janey that was serious enough to warrant her giving me my own key. I didn't think I was that much of a dirtbag to do something like that to my friend Bob, so the fact that my key fit the door must have simply just meant that this was supposed to be my house.

Don't overanalyze things, that's my motto. No wait, that's not my motto at all; my motto is "deny everything." Or is it . . . oh, nevermind.

We made ourselves at home (why wouldn't we?), took showers and grilled some steaks. I discovered that not only did I have cable, but 12 premium channels too, and soon all three of us were relaxing in front of the tube watching *Rocky IV* and downing some cold beers. I felt better than I had in weeks. Clean shaven, well fed, relaxed. Life wasn't so very bad at the moment.

I sure was going to miss that 42" plasma TV though.

Chapter 20

The next day dawned bright and clear. I hate that. One of these days – I swear – I'm gonna move to New Jersey so I can enjoy some good old fashioned gloomy weather. Probably move right next to the Newark airport; just to make sure I get the full "doom" effect.

Simon walked in the kitchen in his boxers and got a cup of coffee. Didn't say a word. I had that going for me anyway. I peeked in the living room and saw Jimmy sleeping on the couch in his favorite ducky underwear. I had plenty of bedroom space (my new house had four in fact), but Jimmy didn't feel comfortable unless sleeping on a couch, floor, or the backseat of a car. I heard him murmur something about "caught in a river riptide" and "washing up on the rocks" and let him be. Went to get a cup of coffee myself. Made sure I turned the damn coffee maker off this time.

I joined Simon on the back porch.

"Well," he said, "what do we do now?"

It was a good question, even if Simon was the one asking. I had been pondering the same thing myself. So many clues. I couldn't make heads or tails of it. Not that you can "make heads or tails" of anything; I mean, if you think about it, it's really a stupid thing to say. Which is why I only think it but never speak it aloud.

"Well, I was watching Nightline last night after you and Jimmy passed out and I got an idea," I said.

"What was it about?" he replied.

"What, the show?"

"Yeah. What happened that gave you the idea."

"Nothing *they* said. It just happened to be on when the idea came to me."

"You're sure?"

"Of course I'm sure."

"Because," he continued, "Ted Koppel's a pretty smart guy. He generally says some pretty insightful things. I just thought that he might have said something that gave you an idea."

"Well, he didn't. I'm my own man."

"Okay, okay, I was just asking."

"No, you don't think I can come up with an idea myself, is that it?"

"I didn't say that."

"Yeah, but you were thinking it."

"No, I wasn't. Look, Dick, you're the smartest person I know besides all of my friends and everyone else I've ever met. I mean that. I was just trying to get a faint understanding of how you do what you do."

"Um-hmm. Sucking up now, aren't you?"

"If you say so," he said. "So, anyway, what was the idea?"

"Well, I think we might just be stuck in the mire of the details a little too deep to see the big picture anymore. I thought it might be a good idea to get another perspective."

"You mean like a 3rd party?"

"Yeah."

"Like a consultant?'

"Yeah, something like that."

"Where are we going to find a consultant who would

be able to help us with this?" Simon asked. "I don't suppose you happen to know one?"

"Oh, I might. I just might indeed."

Saul "The Sandman" Goldblatt arrived promptly at 3 o'clock, just as he promised he would. I call him Sandy. We go way back.

Well, technically that isn't true; he has a suite in my building that he shares with his partners Don Johnson (like the actor, but no relation) and Don's sister Stacy Johnson (like the girl I was hot for in high school, but no relation).

One morning about six months ago I came back from Starbucks and accidentally walked into their office by mistake. I saw the three of them and was so startled I dumped my coffee all over their carpet. Since I thought I was being robbed, and being one who subscribes to the philosophy "shoot first, ask questions later", I also promptly chased them around the room and blew about a dozen holes in their nice paneling (I was carrying a .40 automatic then).

Once things settled down and I realized my mistake, I quickly apologized, and even though I kind of felt they owed me for the coffee, I didn't push it, what with making a mess of their office and almost killing them and all.

Long story short; we got to talking shop, learned a little about each other's business, and have become good friends and allies, though I haven't seen any of them since that day. So you can see why when I got to thinking about hiring a consultant, "Johnson, Johnson, & Goldblatt" immediately came to mind.

I took Sandy into the den and we sat down with

Simon and Jimmy who were eating Apple Jacks right out of the box. Sandy seemed very calm and confident, not like the last time I had seen him when he had been jumping around like a squirrel crossing a 4-lane highway as he had dodged my bullets. I respected the fact that he had obviously taken time to work on his bearing and presentation skills. Professionals do that kind of thing. I gave him a knowing nod.

"Hello Mr. Lassiter," he said.

"Please, call me Dick," I replied.

"Yes, well, Dick then," he said, "what can I do for you today."

"We're looking for some advice – my partners and me – regarding a case we're working on. I thought an outside perspective might shed some light on a few things that we haven't been able to figure out."

"Such as?" he asked.

I laid it all out for him. That dude that came into my office to hire me, the spy moose and his worldwide rampage, Rok Hard and the Barking Spider, the really weird trip to that country where the Dutch people live, the break-in at the shampoo factory and all of the mops that were missing, – no, wait, sorry, that's something completely different – and all of the clues picked up along the way.

"I see," Sandy said when I was finished. I noticed that while he had been holding a notepad and pen the entire time, he hadn't taken a single note during my story. He obviously realized the sensitive nature of the case and opted not to compromise national security by writing any of it down. He probably had a photographic memory and had memorized it all. That would be bitchin'.

"And what areas of the case would you like my firm to provide consulting services for?"

"Well, everything," I said.

"Everything."

"Yup. Everything. The whole shooting match. The whole kit and kaboodle. The whole nine yards. The whole enchilada. The whole – "

"I think I get the picture," he said

"Oh, okay. Yeah, to be completely honest with you Sandy," I continued, "we don't have a clue what's going on with this case. Not a fucking clue."

Jimmy and Simon nodded vigorously.

Saul was silent for a moment, his brow creased in a puzzled expression. "Mr. Lassiter, – "

"Dick."

"Yes, Dick," he said, "I'm a little confused here."

"Boy, do we know *that* feeling," Jimmy chimed in. Simon nodded in agreement, unable to add anything as he had just stuffed another handful of cereal into his mouth.

"Are you asking Johnson, Johnson & Goldblatt to consult with you regarding your investigation," Sandy continued, "or are you asking us to completely *take over* the whole investigation for you?"

"Um," I said, "it would be the second thing you said."

More nods from the nodding fools.

"That seems rather unorthodox, don't you think?"

"Well, yes, in a way, but it's been done before."

"It has," he asked, though in more of a 'repeating the statement in a dubious 'I–don't–believe–it' sort of way than in the more conventional 'asking because I really don't know' sort of way.

"Yes. In fact, I've done it before myself. Twice, if I

remember correctly."

"You have." Again, more of a statement thing.

"Um-hmm," I said, nodding. Jimmy and Simon nodded too. A picture of well-oiled teamwork.

"Could I ask, Mr. Lass – I mean, Dick – how many cases have you worked on in your career as an investigator?"

"Oh, boy, let me see here," I said, looking up into the heavens. "Tough one there. Um, wow, kind of hard to put a handle on it, but if I had to guess – and I'm really stretching here – I'd have to say . . . um. . . two."

"Two."

"Plus or minus one," I concurred.

"Yes, well. You realize this is a little beyond the normal scope of my firm's services, and as such, I'll need to confer with my partners – "

"Dick," Simon rudely interrupted, "it's 7 o'clock."

"Gotcha," I said. "Hey listen Sandy, okay, that sounds fine, you go right ahead. In fact, if you could just do that in the other room – your conferring and proposaling and all – that would be just great, because they're doing a rerun of *Fear Factor* on TNT that we haven't seen – "

"The one where they have to eat bull testicles," Jimmy offered.

" – right now and we've been looking forward to watching it all day, so while we're doing that, you can do, you know, whatever it is that you do and we'll meet back up in a hour or so, okay? Great."

I got up and ushered a confused looking Sandy to the next room while Jimmy and Simon pulled all of the cushions off of the couch searching for the remote control. There was a slight panic when several minutes went by without finding it, but it eventually turned up in the guest bathroom medicine chest.

We settled down in front of the tube and got ready for the first round.

An hour later we had finished cheering the winner and were relaxing in the afterglow of another fine episode when Sandy walked back into the room.

"Alright gentlemen," he said, "I have my recommendations ready."

Now we were getting someplace.

Chapter 21

I popped the top on a cold Bud and watched the foam drip down on the bricks between my feet.

"We're fired?" Jimmy asked. "Can they do that?"

"Apparently they can," Simon replied.

"Fucking consultants," I said, shaking my head in disbelief. "I should have known better. You can't believe a thing they say, the sneaky bastards."

We were all sitting on the front steps of the house, elbows on knees, in dejected shock. The highs and lows of life offer no warning. At least we still had a shitload of beer.

"I've never been fired before," Jimmy said.

Simon snorted. "Jimmy," he said, "you've been fired from every job you ever had."

"I have?"

"Yeah."

"Oh. Wow," Jimmy said. "That would explain a lot."

Following the wise investment of our time in watching good looking guys & gals in spandex do and eat almost anything for the chance at making a couple bucks, Sandy had gutted us like fish with his recommendations. The whole crux of the problem, he had told us, was that we were involved. By taking us out of the equation, there was a much better chance of Zodar actually being caught, even though no one would be looking for him anymore.

To add insult to injury, he charged us $30,000 for his services (which was a little higher than I thought fair) and walked out with our last bag of Cheetos.

"So what now, Dick?" Simon asked.

I didn't have an answer for him. I just stared into the distance and shook my head. I couldn't believe it was over. All the work, all of the time, and for what? Nothing, that's what. Well, okay, I did have a new house. And a nicer car. And pretty close to $200,000 in cash. But other than that, nothing.

The worst part of it was that this moose had gotten into my head. There was something going on, something other than the obvious, and I couldn't figure out what it was. I didn't like that. I felt like the moose was playing me. I didn't like that either. My investigative senses were tingling like crazy, and there wasn't anything I could do about it. All I could do now was walk away.

Or sit here and drink beer. Which we had been doing for a couple of hours now. Lesser of two evils and all that.

"Well, I'm going to go in and catch the news," Simon said. "Tomorrow morning maybe you can give me a lift back up to Wilmington?"

I nodded.

"Yeah dude," Jimmy said, "and if you're heading up that way, I guess I could catch a ride back to my place too? I heard the surf's breaking 3 to 4 feet, which is pretty good for around here."

"Sure Jimmy," I said. "I'll bring you home too."

"Cool," he said, and followed Simon inside, leaving me to my thoughts.

I stared out across the yard, looking at all of the things around me and not really caring about any of them as I once had. The big oak tree by the road that we'd played on as kids, swinging from a rope long since rotted away and diving into the street since there wasn't a pond nearby. Old man Potter's yard, so green and well-manicured that we couldn't help driving our cars over it as teenagers, spewing rooster tails of sod and flowers all over his house until he'd come out, fist raised, so angry that several times he had cardiac arrest and had to be rushed to the hospital. And the sinkhole near the corner that all the kids had pretended was a bomb crater when playing soldiers, all of us jumping bravely into it for cover time and time again until the day Billy Sturgis, wounded by German sniper fire, jumped in and disappeared forever.

Such memories, such good times. Yet I was numb to it all. We were off the case. And knowing that it was my fault just made it worse.

Poor Jimmy and Simon; even though Jimmy still didn't really know what was going on and Simon was only involved because he was afraid of me, their disappointment must rival my own, so obsessed were they in their zeal to see the rogue moose brought to justice.

I took another slug of beer and felt my senses dull a little further as I continued drifting into oblivion. As my eyes roamed mindlessly from one thing to another, they eventually settled on the Porsche, which was parked facing me on top of some hibiscus bushes. I stared at it absently, taking in the yellow hood emblem with the stallion, the front grill, the headlights. An altogether fine looking vehicle. But after a few minutes, something about it seemed not quite right.

I sharpened my gaze to figure out what it was that seemed wrong. There was a dent on the front bumper, but that would have been from the airport when I hit the mechanical arm at the ticket booth. No, as much as the dent detracted from the symmetry of the vehicle, that wasn't it. There was something else, something about the dent, but not the dent itself.

I stood and opened the front door of the house. Stuck my arm through and turned on the porch light. There, now I could see it. The color was different on the dented area, like a smudge of paint. But it couldn't be from the barrier arm at the ticket booth; that had been bright orange. This was a darker color, a dark brown.

I walked over to the car and bent down to get a closer look. Ran my fingernail across the discolored area and examined what came off. It was a smudge alright, but it wasn't paint. It was antler fuzz.

At that moment Simon stuck his head out of the front door.

"Dick," he said, "come in here, now. There's something that you need to see."

I followed Simon into the house, wondering what could be so important that he would actually have the guts to combine telling me to do something with the word "now".

When I entered the living room, both Jimmy and Simon were staring at the TV with wide eyes, the box of Apple Jacks long forgotten on the floor. Before I could say anything, Simon pointed at the TV and said, "Look."

If my mind had already been alarmed at the newly found antler fuzz on the car, it now positively reeled by what I saw.

The camera showed a scene of desolation, brightly lit by powerful floodlights; farmland in South America that now looked like a battleground. Crops flattened and burning, deep furrows dug into the earth, wrecked farm equipment toppled and strewn over the landscape.

My mind only caught snippets of the excited reporter's voice, but it was enough to piece together that this was the work of the spy moose, and that it had occurred just moments before. It was a scene all too familiar; the world had been seeing this type of devastation for months now.

But this time there was more.

The camera and lights bounced excitedly across the field, following the beckoning reporter at a frantic pace. Confusion reigned at the scene, people scampered back and forth across the camera's eye, and shouts & orders crisscrossed through the darkened countryside.

Suddenly, the camera stopped. The reporter stood in front, trying to dominate the scene while pointing and talking in a never ceasing stream. But the camera didn't focus on the correspondent, it ignored him and moved instead to show an area marked off by yellow police tape and guarded by soldiers with very serious looking automatic weapons.

It was clear the guards were not even going to consider allowing anyone to go into the cordoned area, but the camera itself did not know those boundaries, and slowly the picture zoomed past the yellow tape.

A huge animal lay inert on the ground, filthy with dirt and shreds of organic matter, and riddled with bullet holes.

A huge animal with antlers.

Zodar was dead.

Chapter 22

If there was a fan running somewhere in the world, I'm confident that over the next few days the owner was no doubt utterly confounded by the amount of shit hitting it.

We stayed up into the wee hours following the newscasts, which had pre-empted all other programming, including Nightline. Early the next morning, the coverage continued, as it did in fact for days to come as more and more information and details were made available to the public. We followed it all from my living room.

We watched the first daytime footage, in which we were able to see just how much damage the moose had taken. In addition to the thousands of bullet holes, huge tears and gashes in its hide were evident from flying shrapnel, and the left hindquarter had been blown completely off by an anti-personnel mine.

We watched as the country formally known as the USSR issued an apology to the world while the artist formally known as Prince sang *When Moose Cry* to frenzied thousands in Central Park.

We watched as the talking news heads debated what was done, what wasn't done, what should have been done, and whose fault it all was, now that they had the advantage of perfect 20/20 hindsight.

We watched as it was discovered that the spy moose was not in fact a real animal at all, but a machine. A highly specialized robot built specifically for diabolical means.

At this point we ran out of that good cheese dip with the jalapenos in it, and since we were running a little low on beer as well, we decided to make a quick run down to the store, which wound up taking a little longer than we meant it to since Jimmy saw a putt-putt course on the way and threw a fit until we agreed to play a round.

We were having a great time and might have just said to hell with the whole story and not come back at all but of course Simon had to get in an argument with Jimmy over whether or not having your ball hit the windmill did or did not count as a one stroke penalty which escalated into a great clashing of putters and the eventual ejection of all three of us from the course.

So, with nothing better to do, we went back to the house.

We watched as soldiers loaded the mechanized carcass of the moose onto a flatbed truck and drove it to a large airplane hangar in Cartagena where it was lost forever from public sight.

We watched as beer prices dropped to all-time lows now that the threat to crops was over, and how a group of five housewives in Indiana had become millionaires when they'd invested all of their retirement savings into depressed General Mills stock which had now skyrocketed to astronomical heights.

We watched it all. But I didn't believe a word of it. Because I knew something that the rest of the world didn't know. I knew something that just wasn't explained by everything we had seen on the news. Something that told me that the world had been deceived. Something that was on the front of my car.

Antler fuzz.

That, and the fact that all of the commercials I had seen for the Magic Kingdom in the past few days were wrong.

Chapter 23

"I don't understand," said Jimmy. "You mean, we're back on the case?"

"Yes we are," I answered.

"But, I thought they got him. We saw it on TV, the moose is dead."

"That's not the real spy moose," I replied.

We were sitting around my kitchen table, plates from our just finished dinner pushed to the side, discussing our next moves. Simon leaned forward (which was obviously his next move, though we didn't discuss it ahead of time).

"Dick," he said, "fill us in. You apparently know some things you haven't been telling us."

"Indeed I do. But first, I need to know if you're still with me. I need to know if you're going to see this thing through to the end."

"You know we are, Dick," Simon answered, "but how can we? We got fired, remember?"

I did remember. I also remembered that it had been a long, long time since I had lit a cigarette without even thinking about it.

"Did we?" I asked.

"Well, yeah dude," Jimmy said. "You were right there with us."

"Oh, I remember alright," I said, suddenly noticing the lit cigarette in my hand and not having the faintest idea of when I had lit it. "But think about it for a moment. Who fired us?"

"Well, Sandy did," Simon replied.

"That's right. But what is Sandy after all?"

This question seemed to stump them for a moment. Jimmy's guess was "a man", which technically was true, but not the answer I was looking for. Simon eventually got it.

"He's a consultant?"

"Right again," I said. "And what did I tell you about consultants?"

This was a much harder question and took a few minutes. I was surprised when it was Jimmy who came forth with the answer.

"Oooo! Oooo! I know! I know!" he said, wide eyed and jumping up and down. "They're sneaky bastards and you can't trust a thing they say!"

"Good man," I said smiling. "You're right. You're absolutely right. And if you can't believe anything they say, then . . ."

The lightbulb went off in Simon's head first this time.

"Then we can't believe them when they say that we're fired!"

"Correct-a-mundo," I said, enjoying their moment of discovery.

It was a good time to have a beer, so we all opened another one and toasted our good fortune of being employed again. The celebration was short lived, however, as we soon returned to the business at hand.

"Okay," Simon said, "we're back on the case. But are we any further ahead than we were before?"

"Absolutely. A lot has happened since we got fired," I said. "And pieces of the puzzle are finally starting to fall into place."

"Like what?" Jimmy asked.

"Like moose hats and cod stands and trips to Amsterdam. Like a mechanical moose that destroys crops and walks on the ceilings of airplanes and leaves antler fuzz on my car. Like commercials that don't make any sense and a bar that disappears and a chapter of this book that is missing."

"We know all *that*," Simon said, obviously frustrated, "but what does it all mean?"

"I'm not completely sure yet," I said, "but I think we're actually dealing with two mysteries, not one."

"Holy shit, dude," Jimmy said, "you're gonna fry my brain! This is getting *hard*."

"It is complicated," I offered, "and there are a few pieces of the puzzle – or should I say *puzzles* – that are missing. But here's what I think is going on . . . "

After explaining for the next half hour, I sat back and watched Simon stroke his chin in what I can only assume was a thoughtful, introspective manner. Jimmy looked totally confused, so I was pretty sure I had covered everything in full detail.

"Interesting," Simon said. "Outlandish, unbelievable, and totally ridiculous, but interesting."

"Can you go over the second part again dude?" Jimmy asked.

"Sorry Jimmy, we don't have time for that. Things are starting to come to a head and we need to get moving if we're going to get to the bottom of all this in time."

"Yeah, I hear ya dude. A big 10-4 roger wilco on that," he said.

"So what now?" Simon asked.

"Now, I have to make a few phone calls. One to the local public library, and one to the great city of

Montgomery, Alabama."
"And then?"
"Then, we're going out to get a drink."

Chapter 24

We walked into the bar and took three empty stools. Sat in them actually, since it'd be kind of stupid to take them anywhere. I mean, what the hell would you do with them? At any rate, we made ourselves comfortable and waited to be served. After a few minutes, the bartender came down our way.

"Hiya Rok," I said. "Long time."

"Actually, it's only been a couple of weeks," he said.

"Seems longer."

"Yeah. Maybe. What can I do for you tonight?"

I pursed my lips and shrugged. "Just talk."

"'Bout what?" he said.

"I don't know. Maybe a spy moose or two."

"Not much to say. Looks like they got him. And without your help or mine."

"Yeah, well, that's what I wanted to talk to you about. Your help, I mean."

"Look, Dick, this thing is over," he said, resting his anvil sized elbows on the bar. "It was fun while it lasted, but there's no game on anymore. The moose is dead, the jig is up, and that's just how it is. I'm sorry that it wasn't you that got him, but hey, that's your problem, not mine. Now, do you want a beer, or what? I got a business to run here."

"Not anymore Rok."

I saw the first hint of fear in Rok's eyes. He squinted and moved his face a few inches closer to mine.

"Just what are you trying to say?" he said.

"You said it for me, remember? 'The jig is up' are the words I think you used."

"I think it's time for you boys to leave," he said. "Take a look around you. This is a dangerous crowd. Real easy for people to get hurt in here they say the wrong thing. Hurt bad."

"Fair enough," I said, nodding but not moving. "Say, Rok, what's a beer going for around here these days?"

"Huh?"

"A beer, Rok. How much you charging?"

I had pushed him as far as he was going to let me. Now it was time to push him further.

"You're right, Rok. This is a tough crowd in here. Wonder what they'd think if I told them all about how you've been cheating them by jacking up the price of your booze?"

I let that sink in for a moment. As big as Rok was, there was no way he could take on everyone in the bar, and he knew it.

"What do you think Rok? You want to talk to me now?"

Just in case he wasn't thoroughly on board, I directed his gaze to my hand, which was conveniently holding my mini-howitzer, which in turn was conveniently pointed right at his stomach.

"Why don't you three come on in the back," he said.

The situation room looked very much the same, but it was dark and seemed quieter now that it hadn't been used for the past few days. Rok walked wearily to the back of the room and took a seat at the table, a man defeated. In the darkness I could see another figure already seated. I flipped on the light.

"Dickie boy," Stinky Pete said, "How ya doing?"

"Just fine Stinky, just fine."

"I don't suppose this is just a social call to talk about old times, now is it? Who ya got there with you? Couple of federal types?"

"My partners."

"Oh, yeah, I recognize them now. Jimmy the burnout and Simon the Simple. How you boys doing?"

Jimmy seemed delighted to be asked and started to tell them, but Simon jabbed an elbow in his ribs to shut him up.

"Where are my manners?" Stinky said, "Ya'll come over and have a seat, will you? Take a load off and all that."

"We'll stand, thanks," I said, not wanting to get anywhere near the biceps of either Stinky or Rok. I preferred to rely on the 12 feet of open space and the muzzle of my gun between us to keep things cordial.

"Suit yourself," Stinky replied, leaning back in his chair. "So what now?"

"Now I tell you a story."

"Oooo, good, I love stories," Jimmy said.

"Knock it off Jimmy," said Simon.

"It was all very slick," I continued. "I'm really amazed that you guys thought of it. Building a mechanical moose and sending it around the world to destroy every crop known to man. Not for political reasons. Not as an act of terrorism. But for the simple motive that's behind almost every crime ever committed: Money.

"You two figured that if you could drive agricultural production to the brink of extinction, it would force prices of *all* agricultural products sky high. The same agricultural products used in the making of liquor and beer. The world goes hungry, but Rok and Stinky make a killing selling high dollar booze to the same poor saps that they're starving to death. I guess when you get down to it, it's always all about the Jack, isn't it Stinky?"

"It was working too," he said, "and we would have gotten away with it if it weren't for you meddling detectives."

"Duuuuuuuuuude!" Jimmy said, "that is so just like on Scooby Doo!"

"Shut up Jimmy," everyone said in unison.

"So how did you figure it out?" Rok asked.

"Took me a while, I'll admit. But I was trying to figure out one mystery when I actually had clues for two. I couldn't see how they all fit together. The break came when I realized that they *didn't* go together at all."

Stinky nodded at me, then at Rok. "I knew you were going to be trouble the minute you showed up here asking questions. We could've just killed you, Dick. But we never wanted to hurt you; we just wanted to get you out of our way."

"I appreciate that. And I intend to do you the same favor. Not killing you, I mean. All you need to do is give me what I came here for."

"Now, Dick, you know I can't do that."

I raised the barrel of the gun and gave Stinky a good look at it. He reconsidered, as I thought he would.

"Alright, alright," he said. "It's in the desk drawer, over by the computer. Doesn't make much difference now anyway."

I looked at Simon and jerked my head. He walked to

the desk, opened the drawer, took out a manila envelope, and handed it to me. I tucked it away under my trench coat.

"Been nice seeing you again, Dick," Stinky said. "I guess you'll be on your way now. If I ever need you for anything, I'll give you a call."

"Don't bother. I don't work for inmates."

Stinky started laughing. "C'mon, Dick, it's great that you know what happened and all, but you got no *proof*, my friend. And since I don't fancy me or Rok making a confession anytime soon, it's just your word against ours and let's face it, who's gonna believe *you*?"

At that moment the back door crashed open and six men dressed all in black burst through. For a second I thought these might be the same Kung Fu guys from Jimmy's place come back for more (with automatic weapons this time) until I saw Jackson Burroughs walk in the room behind them.

"Nobody needs to believe him, Stinky," he said. "We got it all on tape."

With that, I nodded to Jackson and took my leave.

The parking lot of the Barking Spider looked very much the same as it had last time we were in town. Jimmy & Simon were waiting for me, sitting on the hood of the Impala, which, as it turned out, had been parked here the whole time. We were about to get in when Jackson emerged from the front door of the bar.

"Lassiter," he called out. "Need a word."

I told Jimmy and Simon to get in the car and then walked over to where Jackson was standing.

"Yeah?" I said.

"Listen, I just wanted to say thanks. This whole

thing . . . ," he said, looking away and shaking his head, "it's not what we thought it was at all. Just want to let you know we appreciate your help."

He held out the second manila envelope that I had seen in the past 10 minutes. I took it from him.

"You're welcome," I said, and turned to go.

"Dick, wait," he said. I stopped and turned back to him. Whole lotta turning going on all of a sudden. Almost got dizzy and fell. Didn't though. Wouldn't be cool.

"While you were in there," he continued, "I couldn't help but hear. What did he give you Dick?"

"Nothing important," I said. "Just my bar tab. Want to square my bill."

"Bar tab, huh?" he said, chuckling. "Yeah, okay. Get out of here Lassiter."

I started walking back to the car again but stopped halfway there and looked back.

"Hey Burroughs."

"Yeah?"

"You might want to run a check on that Porsche over there. I got a feeling it's hot."

"Yeah. I'll do that."

The Impala cranked up on the fourth try and we blew out of the parking lot, leaving it covered with a shroud of exhaust.

Chapter 25

Cruising down I-95, top down, heading South. I handed the envelope Burroughs had given to me to Simon. It was full of money. About 300 G's. Payment for services rendered.

I was enjoying the drive; the monotonous drone of the engine, the steady passage of highway, and the cool wind blowing by were all working together in a peaceful alliance until Simon had to fuck it all up by asking questions again. I really had to break him of that habit.

"I still don't understand how you figured it all out," he said. "Can you explain it again? I mean, from the beginning?"

I didn't see much of a reason not to. We had a long drive back to Orlando and I could tell that neither Simon nor Jimmy were going to let me have any solitude. What the hell.

"Stinky Pete and Rok were old war buddies. Rok told me as much when I spoke with him a few weeks ago. They hatched a plan to make some big money, which, as I've already said, involved driving the price of grains up by reducing the amount of grains available. That way, they could charge outrageous amounts of money for the booze they were serving."

"But if the price of grain went up, wouldn't they be paying more for the booze in the first place?" Simon asked, his Ivy League pedigree paying dividends.

"Yes, unless they already had plenty of grain available, which they did. In fact, they bought up several large farms in the Midwest during the past few years. While they were destroying everyone else's crops, theirs remained untouched, and the price skyrocketed."

"Wait a minute. If they already had their grain, then why wouldn't they just make their profit on the grain itself, rather than on the secondary product of booze? Isn't that kind of stupid?"

"Hey, it was their plan, not mine."

"Oh, yeah. Sorry."

"Anyway, the problem they ran into was how to wreak that much havoc in the agricultural community without getting caught. During their years in covert field ops, they had heard rumors of this spy moose that the Soviets had dreamed up. The Cold War was long over and no one had seen or heard anything about Zodar in years, so they decided to make their own. That way, not only would it look like someone else was destroying all of the crops, it would look like there was a completely different reason for *why* they were being wiped out."

"Clever," Simon said. "But why did Stinky Pete disappear?"

"He didn't. Someone had to operate the moose, so Stinky took off around the world to do that while Rok stayed back at the bar and started turning the profit. Say Jimmy, are you going to Bogart that whole bag of Doritos back there or what?"

"Oh, sorry dude," Jimmy said, passing the bag up to the front.

"No problem," I said, popping a couple chips in my mouth. "Anyway, they knew that since they were using an old Soviet weapon as their angle, the spooks would eventually get involved, and that there was a good possibility that they'd come looking to me for help. Stinky knew that I'd then come looking to him for some intel, so they torched the Roadkill and had it paved over to throw me off of their track. And it probably would've ended right there except that by sheer luck we wound up at the Barking Spider, where Stinky's partner Rok is holding down the fort and coordinating Zodar's strikes."

"How did you figure that out?" Simon asked.

"It was the pins on the map of the world back in the situation room, although I didn't notice it 'till later. Rok said he was tracking where the spy moose had already struck, but there were pins on several countries that Zodar hadn't hit yet, including Columbia. Zodar didn't go there until we were in Amsterdam."

"Well that's kind of bullshit," Simon said.

"Huh? What're you talking about?"

"You didn't tell anybody about any pins that were marked on countries that Zodar hadn't been to yet."

"Yeah, so?"

"Well, it's a bullshit clue. How are we supposed to figure out the mystery if you don't give us all of the clues? I mean, it's great that you knew that, but it doesn't do anybody else any good."

"Hey, lay off, will ya? Sherlock Holmes did that shit all the time. It's absolutely acceptable."

"Well, last I checked, this ain't no Sherlock Holmes."

"I swear Simon, I'm gonna just pop the fuck out of you if you don't lay off. Here I am, busting my ass and making you two look good in the process, and I'm catching grief? You kidding me?"

Simon crossed his arms and stuck out his lower lip.

"Just seems kind of unfair is all," he said.

"You want fair? Play a fucking board game."

"Um, hey," Jimmy said cautiously. "What was the whole Amsterdam trip thing about anyway?" asked Jimmy. "What did we go there for?"

"To get us out of the way, pure & simple. I mean, what the hell do they grow in Amsterdam, right? Rok got us all drunk, put us on the plane, and then came along to give us some false clues so we'd think we were heading in the right direction."

"You mean . . ."

"That's right, he planted the hoof prints on the ceiling of the plane. And when I got too close to him back in the coach section, he clocked me a few times to keep me from getting a good look at him."

"Makes sense," said Simon. "Who better to navigate through the coach class of an airplane than someone skilled in jungle warfare."

"Exactly."

"But it was us that destroyed those dude's country, right?" asked Jimmy.

"Not a chance, my friend," I replied. "Remember the little guy you popped in the nards with your board? We assumed that he was the one holding back the dyke with his finger, and that by taking him out of action, the dyke burst. But c'mon, think about it. Holding back millions of gallons of water with your finger? He was just a tourist attraction, that's all."

"But then how . . ." Jimmy started.

"Let me guess," Simon said. "Rok again."

"Bingo. Rok blows the dyke, we take the fall, and the next thing you know we're tucked away all nice & tidy in a Dutch jail as far from the action as we can get, and no one has any idea that we're there."

"But someone *did* know we were there," Jimmy said. "That dude that bailed us out."

"Mr. I.P. Freeley," I said, nodding.

"Hey," said Jimmy, "is he the dude that wrote – "

"*The Yellow River*, yes."

"Wow, that was a great book," Jimmy said. "I didn't know that was him. I would've got his autograph. He really wrote good stuff."

"That's not all he did," I said. "Remember that call I made to the library? I did a little background on *The Yellow River* and guess what I found? Turns out that the first edition was printed in Russian. After that I talked to that nice lady in Montgomery, AL again, and after she finally transferred me to Burroughs, I got some more information on Mr. Freeley. Seems he was on staff at the Central Moscow Community College at the same time our friend Zodar was."

"You mean – "

"That's right. Freeley helped *train* Zodar."

It was quiet for a moment while that sunk in. Then Simon asked the obvious question.

"But why would Freeley help us? And how did he know we were there?"

"Good question. And I couldn't for the life of me figure that one out. Until I realized that the Zodar we were after wasn't what we thought he was. As it turns out, Zodar – the *real* Zodar – was keeping an eye on us all along. Following us around. He was at the airport in Amsterdam disguised as a cod vendor, and again in Orlando disguised as the barrier arm, the one we hit with the Porsche, remember? Zodar had Freeley bail us out.

"The final piece that put it all together for me was the antler fuzz on the bumper. Zodar *couldn't* have been in South America and Orlando at the same time, and yet I had evidence to that effect. That's when it hit me that there must be *two* Zodars running around."

"Cool, dude," said Jimmy. "Well, I guess that takes care of that. Hey, you pass the chips back here again?"

"Wait a minute," Simon said. "That explains *one* of the Zodars – the fake one – but what about the *real* one? Why was he following us around? Why did he get us bailed out when we got thrown in jail? What is *he* up to?"

"Actually, I figured that out a long time ago."

Simon shot me a look. "What are you talking about?"

"Like I said. I already figured out what he's doing."

"Were you planning to share any of that information with us?"

"Of course."

"Okay," he said after a few moments went by. "I guess this would be as good a time as any. Let's hear it."

"I can't tell you."

"*What?*"

"I said, 'I can't tell you'. Really, Simon, clean the wax out of your ears."

"I *know* what you said, but *why* can't you tell us?"

"Because I don't know."

"What do you mean you don't know? You just said you figured it out a long time ago."

"I did."

"Then what is he doing?"

"I don't know. Come on Simon, this isn't that difficult to understand."

Simon looked at me hard for a minute. "Okay, let's

say for a second that it is difficult to understand and that I happen to be the type of person who doesn't do well with difficult things. In other words, pretend I'm Jimmy."

"Duuuuuude," Jimmy said, "that is so cool. There's gonna be *two* of me. This'll be *righteous* dude. You're gonna be like 'Oh, man, it's so cool to be Jimmy'. And we can hang out together and order pizza and be pals and stuff. I'll teach you how to surf and – "

"Jimmy, will you *shut up*!" Simon yelled.

Jimmy sunk back into the seat, a hurt look on his face. Simon let out an exasperated yet slightly sympathetic sigh, and after a moment of tense silence, tried his best to patch things up. With Jimmy, this isn't really hard.

"Look," Simon said, "I think that's a great idea. But how about for our first 'pal' thing, we play The Silent Game. You know, where we see who can go the longest without saying anything?"

"Okay," Jimmy said, already noticeably happier. Simon turned his attention back to me.

"Alright, Dick, what's –"

"Duuuuuude, you lose!" Jimmy said excitedly.

"*We haven't started playing yet!*" Simon yelled back.

"Oh," said Jimmy.

Simon took a deep breath. "Talk to me Dick," he said to me. Then to Jimmy, "Now we're playing."

"Okay," I said. "I figured the whole thing out back at the Barking Spider."

"But we were just there," Simon replied. "You didn't say anything."

"I win! I win!" Jimmy yelled to no one in particular. "I am the greatest of all time!"

"Not *then*," I continued, ignoring Jimmy, "the *first*

time we were there. After you and Jimmy were passed out. Something happened; I saw something, or heard something – I don't know which – and figured out what was going on. The problem is, Rok knew I had figured it out too. And he realized that if I knew what was going on with the *real* Zodar, the fake Zodar would be unmasked as a phony and their cover would be blown."

"So?" asked Simon.

I pulled out the manila envelope that Stinky Pete had given me and placed it on the seat.

"So that's why he stole Chapter 10."

Chapter 10

Someone had poured glue in my mouth and hit me in the head with a pipe. Stainless steel schedule 80 by the feel of it. My arms felt like they were full of angry bees and my stomach was currently on spin cycle. To top it all off, I was blind – which was bad – although my sense of smell seemed to be just fine. Normally I would consider that a good thing, but judging from the smell of the fart that ripped out of my butt I wasn't so sure, since it seemed to indicate that a small woodland animal had decided to take up residence in my colon and then promptly die there. This kind of thing didn't happen when I was nineteen.

The angel of death approached and extended a fist towards me.

"Here," Rok said. "Eat these."

I held out my hand and accepted the offering. Like I was gonna say 'no'. I took a moment to consider what to do with the half pound of pills, capsules, lozenges and suppositories that I was now holding when Rok placed a glass of water in my other hand. I had almost made the connection of what I was supposed to do when he spoke again.

"Come on, knock 'em back. They'll make you feel better." Rok turned and walked back to the other side of the room.

I glared at him for a moment. I would have figured it out myself eventually. Oh, well. I started to lift the pills to my mouth when he suddenly turned.

"Hey, is there a little white capsule in there?" he asked.

I looked. There was.

"Yeah," I said.

"Okay. Hey, don't eat that one okay?"

"Why not?"

"It's a suicide pill. Cyanide. You'd be dead in 15 seconds. Flat."

"Oh," I said, plucking the intruder from the rest of the pills. "Good safety tip. Anything else in here that might be a surprise?"

"Nah. Not that I can think of anyway."

I put the cyanide pill in my pocket for safe keeping. Wouldn't want the little rascal to accidentally find its way into someplace dangerous, like, say, my stomach. The rest of the pills looked fairly pharmaceutical so I swallowed them one by one and hoped for the best.

When I had finished, Rok was sitting at one of the computer terminals typing frenetically. Or possibly frantically, it was too early to tell. Either something had happened or the deadline for submissions to this month's Penthouse Forum was almost at hand.

"What's going on?" I said as I struggled to my feet.

"Bad things. My contact in Japan has identified some local activity from our four legged friend."

I scratched my head. "He's in Japan? I thought he was in Europe somewhere."

"He *is* in Europe. In Norway? You know, the country right across the border from Japan?" Rok sighed. "Duh."

Yeah. Okay. This all made sense.

I pulled out a cigarette and fired it up. It was nice for a change to consciously do this, although where I got a gold Zippo with "ZSM" engraved on it I had no idea. I took the last drag and ground the cigarette out on the floor. Time had no relevance here.

"So, Rokko, are you going to fill me in here or what? All that typing you're doing, there must be some major communication going on."

"Yeah, just finishing up. Let me print it out for you." A few more keystrokes and several sheets of paper spewed from the laserjet. Rok picked them up and handed them to me. "See what you make of that," he said.

I sat back in the heated La-Z-Boy, kicked my shoes off, took a sip from my Martini, and began to enter the mind of my foe.

I've enjoyed reading the stories in your magazine for years, but I never thought they were true. Until recently that is. It happened on a Tuesday night several weeks ago. I'm a college freshman, and I was in the dorm working diligently on my chemistry assignment when an insistent knocking on the door interrupted my studies. I opened the door slowly and much to my surprise, two of the hottest looking ladies I have ever seen walked on in, devilish smiles on their faces. Tight jeans and tighter sweaters let me know right away that their bodies were made to please. As it turned out, Tracy and Lori (not their real names, of course) had seen me in class, and decided that they were going to unofficially welcome me to the university. . .

My foe was a pervert. I must have been as well because by this point I was well entrenched in the story and a Boy Scout troop had apparently erected a pup-tent in my pants. I read it to the end, when Bill (not his real name either), Tracy, and Lori lay sweaty and exhausted on the floor. I let out a long, satisfied breath.

"Well. What do you think?" Rok said.

"Not bad. But I don't think you explained very well when exactly it was that Lori pulled off her sweater."

Rok blushed and grinned slyly. "Uh," he said, "sorry. Wrong stuff." He snatched the papers from me and turned back to the computer. His fingers flew over the keyboard for a few more seconds and the printer spat out a single sheet. "Here, try this."

By now the Boy Scout troop had broke camp and I was back to business again. I perused the sheet Rok had handed me. It was much shorter and not nearly as sensual as what I had read before, but at least it was applicable to the story. It read:

Roses are red,
Violets are blue,
I destroyed all the crops in Asia,
And now I'll destroy all of the crops in Europe as well.

I reread the note again and pondered it thoughtfully. I don't think you can ponder something any other way, but maybe I'll try later. I knew one thing for sure: Zodar couldn't rhyme worth a shit. Other than that, the message was hazy. What was he trying to say? Rok broke my reverie.

"Interesting, isn't it?"

"Oh yes. Tells us a lot. Like the fact that he's going to destroy all of the crops in Europe. Of course, we already knew that he was in Europe and we already knew what he was going to be doing while he was there, but if we pretended we didn't, this would be big."

"No, not that. You can't take the rhyme literally, it's coded. Means nothing as it is."

"But. . . ," I said, leading him on.

"But if you take every third consonant and multiply the numerical alphabetical value of each by the square root of today's day, date, and year and then assign word values based on a coded index which, in this case, is found on page 78 of the March issue of GQ, you get the baseplate data from which you can then extrapolate the other consonants and all of the vowels and find the *real* message."

"Ah, yes. So simple."

"Yeah. He obviously wanted us to crack it or he would've made it a little harder."

"Obviously," I replied. I looked around for a few moments. "Darn it, would you believe I don't have my March GQ? I was sure I just had it. Say, Rok, could you . . I mean . . . since you've already done the math . . ." I held out the message to Rok. If I hinted any harder I'd break his nose.

"Oh yeah, no sweat." Rok grabbed the note and scribbled underneath it for a few moments. He handed it back.

Of course he handed it back. What the hell else was he going to do with it?

For the third time this morning – which is about three times more often than I prefer in any one month – I began to read:

Good day Mr. Lassiter! And it will always be Mr. Lassiter to me, for I am no friend, nor will I ever be.

At least he was rhyming better.

My mission is a simple one: Revenge! Revenge against those who created me, for creating me to do battle and then pushing me aside once my reason for being no longer existed. Revenge against those for whom my creators had created me to do battle against, for no longer providing my creators with someone to do battle against and thus causing my reason for being too no longer exist and subsequently then giving them reason to push me aside. And revenge against everyone else, for looking like either those who created me or those who I was created to do battle against, just to make sure I don't miss anybody. Okay, I'll admit, it's a tad more complicated than I originally made it out to be, and I apologize if I misled you a little bit.

Nevertheless! That is my mission! Again, in summary for those of you who may still be a little confused: Revenge against the world!

Sincerely,
Zodar the Spy Moose, Esq.

P.S. – By the way, I don't have anything to do with that whole "crop annihilation" thing that's going on. That's just some whacked out scheme that Rok and Stinky Pete thought up to get rich. My nefarious goal is a little loftier; I'm taking over Disney World!

P.S.S. – I look forward to crushing you with my mighty antlers.

I lowered the note.

"Strong words," Rok said.

"Yeah."

Rok poured something into his mouth, noticed me looking at him, and held his hand out to me. "Chiclet?"

"No thanks. Bad memories for me there."

"Suit yourself. I think they're great."

"Depends on your past, I guess."

I straightened my jacket and donned my hat. I love donning my hat. Love it so much I did it again. And then two more times. Getting my instincts back. Felt good.

"Listen, Rok," I said, "we've got a little bit of a problem here."

"Yeah?"

"Yeah. Little bit."

He was now seated at the table, quietly filling a couple dozen shot glasses lined up in front of him with scotch.

"I figured we might. Let me guess. Note tip you off?"

"You could say that."

"Yeah. In hindsight I guess it probably would have been better not to have included that part about me and Stinky Pete, what with me doing the translating and all."

"Probably."

He continued filling the shot glasses until all were full. Then sat back and put the bottle on the table and looked at me.

"You know, Dick," he said, "I wish it didn't have to be like this. I was just starting to like you."

"I appreciate that. But it's a little late for that now."

"Yeah, I know. That's why I'm gonna have to ask you to drink these."

I had a faint idea of what he was planning, but I had absolutely no intention of allowing it to happen.

"And if I say no?" I asked.

"Then I'm gonna have to wrap my biceps around your head and crush your skull."

Hair of the dog or crushed skull. Intentions be damned. Suddenly, having a drink didn't seem like such a bad idea after all. Besides, it had to be 5 o'clock somewhere in the world.

I sat down at the table across from Rok, looked him straight in the eye, and drank the first shot.

Chapter 26

"I can see now why it was important for them to steal that chapter," Simon said. "We would have solved this a long time ago. What a horrible thing for them to do."

"I know," I said, "and all to keep their sordid scheme of quick riches alive at the expense of mankind's suffering."

"No, that's not what I meant. We could've had this book wrapped up by the end of Chapter 13 and been out of here."

We were back at my house, resting in the living room after the nine hour drive. I had been trying to figure out why you got so tired from driving when all you're really doing is just sitting there when Simon had spoken. Since I had just recently scaled back from two mysteries to one, I decided that taking mysteries one at a time was okay with me and left the "tired from driving" puzzle for a later date. Maybe it would turn into a future employment opportunity.

"Nah, the book would've been too short. Wouldn't have even been worth printing," I said.

"All the better for us, I say," Simon replied.

"Be that as it may, we still have work to do. There's a spy moose on the loose and he's up to some serious no good. All the clues point to it."

"Point to what?" asked Simon. Then to Jimmy, "Hey, can you break away from Cartoon Network for just a moment and help us out here?"

Jimmy broke his mind meld with the TV and looked

over. "What?"

"Nevermind," said Simon. "It was a stupid question."

"Yeah, dog," Jimmy said smiling, "you're getting into the whole 'Jimmy' thing now, aren't you? Pretty cool, huh?"

"Oh, shut up."

Jimmy nodded and re-glued his eyes to the tube, still smiling his silly smile. "Yeah, dog."

"I think we're just going to have to do without the aid of surfer boy," Simon said to me.

I nodded. "Probably be faster that way."

"So bring me up to date on Zodar," Simon said. "Having now read Chapter 10, I can see how that would have compromised Rok and Stinky Pete, but what leads do we have on the moose himself?"

"He's after Disney World. Wants to replace the mouse with the moose."

"But how do you know for sure?"

"Think about it. Cod stands, much like the turkey leg vendors they have at the Magic Kingdom, but with a more Siberian flair. Moose hats appearing worldwide as tourists recently returning from our fair vacationland carry home souvenir hats graced not with familiar round mouse ears, but instead by big fuzzy antlers. And theme park commercials bombarding the airwaves featuring Mickey and Minnie waving gaily to the television audience."

"Hold on. I can see the evil workings afoot in the cod stands and hats, but what's so odd about the commercials?'

"Mickey has antlers."

"Oh. I didn't notice."

"No doubt has anyone else. Yes, it's a subtle game he's playing. A game of methodical, subliminal replacement, so smooth that by the time he has replaced Mickey altogether, no one will even remember that there was ever anything *but* a moose."

"The horror," Simon whispered, aghast.

"Yes. With control of the largest entertainment empire in the world, his influence on the masses will be unstoppable. He'll control the world."

"But can you be sure, Dick?" Simon asked. "I mean, sure, the clues all point to it, but can you be *sure*?"

"Well," I said, "in addition to the clues, there was also that little part where he told us, and I quote, '*I'm taking over Disney World*', unquote. So, yeah, I'm pretty sure."

We sat in silence for a while as I let Simon come to grips with the true magnitude of the situation and feel the troubling weight that I myself had been dealing with all by myself for the last five minutes or so. I share like that. Kind of guy I am.

"Well," Simon said at last, "we've got to stop him."

"Duh. You think?"

"Absolutely! Where's the phone?" he said, jumping up and looking around. "We need to call the police, the Army, the Feds; hell, *everybody*! We need to get moving *now*!"

"Hold on there, oh mighty Simon," I said. "We're calling nobody."

"*What?* Are you *kidding* me? C'mon, Dick, we're gonna need help on this."

"And who's gonna believe you? The Feds? The police? What are you going to tell them? There's *another* spy moose on the loose? No, Simon. This one is all us. We're not going to get any help."

"Besides," I said, " this is personal."

"What are you talking about?"

"Why do you think Zodar's been keeping an eye on us? Helping us out even?"

Simon thought for a moment. "Well," he said, "I don't know."

"Hey, what are you guys talking about?" asked Jimmy, finally free from the hypnotic spell of animated existence.

"Zodar," I told him.

"Oh, that guy?" Jimmy said. "I thought we were done with that."

"I'm afraid not, Jimmy."

"Oh, okay," he said. "Hey, I know. I'll get some chips." He bounded off to the kitchen, obviously upset with the peril at hand.

I turned back to Simon. "Zodar's a creation of the Cold War. He was trained to function by Cold War guidelines. And even though the Cold War is long over, he can't break from the rules of engagement that it was played by."

Jimmy came back in and sat on the couch. "Pretzel?"

"Thanks, but not now," I said.

"I'll have some," Simon said.

"Duuuude," Jimmy said, smiling again. "You're getting it. I can tell."

"Jimmy," I said, not hiding my annoyance, "I was right in the middle of a very important and dramatic explanation here. Do you mind?"

"Oh. Sorry," he said. "Go ahead."

I continued while Simon and Jimmy munched away.

"Like I was saying," I said, "Zodar is driven by Cold War tactics. Action and reaction. Bluff and counter bluff. He's playing a game of cat & mouse, but there's no cat. That's why he's been helping us. He needed us to clear up the *fake* Zodar and stop Rok & Stinky so we could focus on *him*. He needs a cat."

"Well, hell," Jimmy said, "we can get him a cat. That's easy. There's cats all over the place. My mom's got four or five – "

"Not a housecat Jimmy," I said.

"Oh," he said. "What then? Like, a lion or something?"

"No, *us* Jimmy. *Us*."

"Dude. That's just weird."

Thankfully Simon jumped in and brought a ray of sanity back into the conversation.

"I follow you, Dick," he said. "It's just him and us now.

"Exactly," I said.

"But what are we supposed to do now? We know what he's trying to do, and we have a fairly good if somewhat ludicrous idea as to how he's doing it. But how do we stop him? We don't even know where he's at."

"Of course we do," I said.

"We do?" Simon and Jimmy chimed in unison.

"Absolutely. He's here. In Orlando."

"Okay, that narrows it down some. But Orlando's still a pretty big place."

"Right, but we don't have to search blindly."

"What do you mean?" Simon asked.

"Zodar has two weaknesses, remember? One is that

whatever he turns into, he can't hide his antlers. The other is that he has a soft spot for women."

"Yeah, so?"

"Well, other than being a land of theme parks, what else is Orlando known for?"

"Um . . . . roads?" said Jimmy. "No wait; grass."

"Beaches," Simon guessed.

"No, gentlemen," I said. "*Think.*"

They did. Paint dried. Seasons turned.

Then suddenly, both of their eyes grew wide as saucers and they blurted out together –

"Strip Clubs!"

"Exactly," I said.

"My God," Simon said to Jimmy, "I am starting to think like you."

"Duuuuuuuuuuude."

Chapter 27

We made it down to the Trail to begin our search, but not before we were subjected to some amount of mental trauma. As we were pulling out of my driveway we saw Bob and Janey Mitchell standing in their front yard, looking in shock at what was left of their home. What a way to return from a vacation. One minute you're simultaneously relieved and excited that you're just around the corner from home, and the next you're weeping in agony with painful spasms wracking your body as you realize that everything you've ever worked for is now a heap of ashes and charred wood. Tragedy has no timing.

My heart went out to them, and I wanted to stop and offer what comfort I could, but then I remembered we had to go strip club hopping so I floored it and we blew past them down the street.

Luck was with us on our first stop. It was a dive called "My Fair Lady". Fair to poor would've been less misleading, but I doubted the management was open to suggestions, so I kept that to myself. After paying our cover we walked in and acclimated ourselves to the strip club funk; that effervescent mix of stale smoke, flat beer, and the universally recognized cheap perfume worn by strippers everywhere. We stood for a few minutes as our eyes adjusted to the dark and the funk permeated our clothes.

"I don't see a moose anywhere," Simon said.

"That's because we aren't looking for a moose," I

replied.

"Dude, you're confusing me again," Jimmy complained.

"Just watch the strippers, Jimmy," I said, "I'll let you know if I find what I'm looking for."

A few seconds later, I let him know.

"Over there," I said with a nod of my head, "sitting up front by the stage."

"The guy with the antlers sticking out of his head?" asked Simon.

"The same."

"Honestly Dick, I don't know how you do it. I never would've noticed."

"It takes a keen eye," I replied. "Look you two, I don't know what's going to happen here. I'd rather you stay back." I dug into my wallet and handed Simon a dollar. "Why don't you guys take a seat at the bar."

Simon looked at the bill in his hand. "Gee, with this plus twenty bucks of our own money, we might have enough for a couple of drinks."

"Don't mention it."

I started across the room slowly. Checked out the exits. Possible escape routes. Weapons of convenience. All the while keeping Zodar in my sights. Other than the headgear, you wouldn't know him from any other average Joe. Sipping his drink. Smoking a cigarette. Checking out the girls.

He was smooth, I'll give him that.

The seat to his right was empty. I took it, sat down, and leaned back. Slow and cool. We sat like that for a while. Just watching the strippers. Taking an occasional draw on a cigarette.

It's always amazed me how much strip joints play into our lives. Movies and books – as honest in their reflection of society as could be possible – constantly make the point. Every time you turn around there's a scene that, for no other reason than the fact that there could be no other way, had to take place in a titty bar. You think I'm kidding? Try finding a movie or a book that doesn't have a strip joint in it. Easier said than done.

Even *The Goodbye Girl* has a scene that takes place in a strip club. Now there's a movie that certainly didn't need one; I mean it's all about love and stuff and even has a little girl in it. She's not the actual 'Goodbye Girl', she's her daughter. The little girl, I mean. But still.

It sure doesn't seem like there's that many strip joints around, but after watching a few flicks, reading a few books, you discover just how much of our nation's history has played out within their windowless walls. And here was yet another crisis of global importance about to play out in those same confines.

The girl on stage in front of me wasn't in any way remarkable, other than the fact that she didn't have any clothes on and seemed to be somewhat infatuated with a vertical pole running from stage to ceiling. And how many times aren't we subjected to that in everyday life that it has now become commonplace?

I didn't know her name, obviously – she had no name tag and where would she put it if she did? – but I figured it was probably Portia. There's always a Portia. Always. I'm not kidding. Next time you're in a strip club, just tell somebody that you're there to see Portia. You won't go away disappointed. Well, if it turns out she's a real schnauzer you might. Unless you're into that kind of thing, not that it's any of my business. Point is, there'll be a Portia.

In the end, it was Zodar who broke the tension. And people say there isn't a God.

"I've been waiting for you," he said.

Good opening line. Wish I'd have thought of it. But oh no, I'm explaining stripper names to you when I could've been thinking of something to say.

"That makes two of us," I replied, instantly regretting it since it sounded cool but didn't make a damn bit of sense.

"Wait a minute," I said quickly, "I take that back. Just forget I said it. Try this instead."

I took a moment to light another cigarette and let the tension build up again. Then I exhaled towards Portia, hoping it would make her back off and go begging for dollars from somebody else.

"Been looking for ya," I said finally.

He nodded thoughtfully, no doubt realizing that I was a serious player.

"I'd like to thank you for taking care of that situation with those two soldiers," he said.

"Who? Oh, you mean Rok and Stinky."

"Yes, I believe that was what they called themselves."

"No problem. Just a couple of dirtbags. Mind you, I got no beef with someone maybe bending the rules a little in the name of making a buck – legal or otherwise – but you start messing with the price of a working man's drink, I'm gonna take exception."

"You're a man of uncommon moral fiber. That's rare these days."

"I'll have to agree on both counts" I said, glancing

around the room. "Hey, check out the hooters on that chick over there, will ya? Holy cow, those babies'll remind you you're a man, huh?"

A moment of uncomfortable silence suddenly fell between us.

"Er . . . sorry. No offense," I said.

"None taken."

"Say, uh, can I ask you a question?"

"Certainly."

"You sure you're not Austrian? I only ask because you sound an awful lot like that Schwarzenegger guy. You know, the body builder? Did some movies?"

"*The Terminator.*"

"Yeah, that's one of 'em. Cool flick. Funny you should mention that one; I used to have some sunglasses just like the ones he wore in that. Supposed to stop a .22 caliber round somebody told me. Like, a lot of good that'll do you, right? I mean, if somebody's shooting at you, what're the odds that they're using a .22, and even if they were, I think I'd want a little more body armor than a pair of sunglasses, you know? And are we talking .22 short, or .22 long – it makes a difference – although I'd have to guess .22 short since – "

"I am definitely Russian," Zodar said.

"Oh," I said. "Yeah, well, like I was saying, you sound just like Schwarzenegger, and *he's* Austrian so I thought maybe you were too."

"I am most definitely not. And, by the way, what makes you so sure that he is?"

"Well," I said, "because . . . . .Oh, GET OUT! He's *Russian*? He *can't* be. He's the President of California for crying out loud."

"Governor."

"Well, yeah, for now maybe, but what then?"

My mind was reeling from what Zodar had just said. Could it be true? Or could it be *True Lies*? New pain shot through my skull and I tried to shake off that horribly cheap pun, not believing that I had just thought it. I did my best to re-center myself, remembering that I was in dangerously close quarters with a moose that was specifically created for intellectual warfare. I realized that I was saying 'I' a lot and wondered if this was but more cerebral fallout caused by an adversary that I had sorely underestimated.

The stress of this battle of wits was tearing me apart, eating away at my sanity, and I wasn't sure how much longer I could handle it. In an attempt to pull myself out of my downward spiral, I tried to envision my potter's wheel and a few pounds of wet clay to ease the tension. It took everything I had to concentrate on the image of that spinning, shimmering clay, and that laser focus, plus my physical exhaustion from driving all day, relaxed me so much that I flat dozed off for a few minutes.

I awoke to Simon's urgent shaking.

"Dick, Dick," he said. "What happened? Are you okay?"

Still dazed, with half open eyes, I looked to my left. The seat was empty. Zodar was gone.

"Must've given me the slip," I said, re-taking in my surroundings. Initially, everything appeared as it was before. But then I noticed that there was a new stripper on stage.

Portia was gone too.

Chapter 28

As a general rule, strippers have a tendency to complicate things, and the abduction of a stripper, especially when done by a four legged mammal with no political ties, has a tendency to really screw shit up. Anyone who's seen *Pretty Woman* will know exactly what I mean.

You see, now it wasn't just Dick, Simon & Jimmy against Zodar the Spy Moose; it was Dick, Simon & Jimmy against Zodar the Spy Moose and Portia. And I know that may seem obvious to you in hindsight, but believe me, there's always an idiot or two out there (Simon and Jimmy would easily cover the spread on that just by themselves) who need it spelled out for them.

Note here too that while Portia isn't technically *against* us, she's still *with* Zodar – whether willingly or not – and if she catches a bullet or two by being there then maybe she should have thought about that ahead of time and gotten a job at Burdines or something rather than at a strip joint where you're just asking to be kidnapped by rogue animals from the former Soviet Union. I mean, talk about Self Preservation 101.

Duh.

Although Portia and I had a history together, I couldn't let that stand in the way of justice. Sure, I couldn't help but remember that morning I woke up to find her nestled softly in my arms, and the way that I frantically tried to gnaw my arm off so that I could escape without waking her, and the way she woke up anyway and . . .

. . . wait . . . wait a minute. That wasn't her. That wasn't her at all. Sorry, sorry, I've got her completely mixed up with somebody else. But I think that in itself is enough to clearly illustrate how strippers complicate things.

We were on Interstate 4, heading West. At least, we were *trying* to head West. What we were actually doing was sitting pretty still in the Westbound lanes, the Impala doing a reasonable if not thoroughly convincing job of impersonating a parked car. But if & when we finally did start moving, I was 90% certain that it would be in a Westerly direction. Because there was only one place that Zodar would go with a hooker.

"I thought she was a stripper," Jimmy asked.

"What?" I said.

"I thought Portia was a *stripper*," Jimmy replied.

"Yeah, so?"

"You just said she was a hooker."

"No I didn't," I said.

"Sure you did. I just heard you."

"No you didn't."

"Did too."

"Did not."

"Did too."

"No, you *didn't*," I said. "You're listening in to my thoughts again is what you're doing. And I already told you to knock that off or I'd pop you one."

"Dick," Simon interjected, "don't get defensive. After all, you were thinking rather loudly. I heard you too. And whether or not that's right or wrong, you *did* call her a hooker."

"Okay, okay," I said, throwing up my hands in exasperation. "Jimmy & Simon, Attorneys at Law. I throw myself on the mercy of the court for crying out loud. Excuse me for making a mistake."

"Well, we probably wouldn't even have mentioned it, but you've made a couple of them lately," Simon said.

"Yup," said Jimmy, nodding.

"What the hell are you two talking about?" I asked.

"Just that you're making some mistakes is all," Simon said. "Some mental mistakes."

"Brain farts," Jimmy added.

"Oh yeah?" I asked. "Like what?"

"Like *Pretty Woman*," Simon answered.

"Okay. What about it?"

"Well, for one thing, nobody in that movie got abducted by a four-legged mammal. At least, I don't think anybody did," Simon said.

"Nope, nope, nobody," said Jimmy shaking his head instead of nodding for a change.

"And Julia Roberts played a *hooker*, not a stripper, so even if a four-legged mammal had kidnapped someone, it's still a moot point."

"Moot," said Jimmy, nodding once again and probably wondering what the hell 'moot' meant, "Definitely moot."

"Wait a minute," I said, "you bozos just jumped all over me because I said she was a hooker and you insisted she was a stripper. Now you saying it's the other way around."

"No, no, no," Simon countered, "*Portia* is the stripper,

Julia Roberts is the hooker."

"She is? No shit?"

"No, in the *movie,* Dick."

"Movie? You mean *The Goodbye Girl*? She wasn't in that." I took a deep breath, pressed my hands to my temples, and sighed loudly. "You guys are messing me up. I can't keep all this straight."

"That's what we're trying to tell you," Simon said, "You're making mental errors. It's just very obvious to us because we've never seen you do that before."

"What about that time at the donut shop?" Jimmy asked Simon.

"Well, yes, there was that," Simon replied to Jimmy, "But usually we don't see him making those kinds of errors. At least not all the time. That's the point I was trying to make."

"Oh. Okay," said Jimmy.

"You guys are whacked," I said, getting annoyed. "*My* thinking is just fine. As long as I don't listen to either of *you*, I know exactly what I'm doing."

"Really?" asked Simon. "Then what are we doing here?"

"We're going to Disney. That's where Zodar will be."

"I see," said Simon. "Then why are we on I-4?"

"I just told you. Because . . ."

My God, he had me. I *was* making mental errors. Why was I on I-4? Certainly not because I had any intention of going anywhere. Only tourists make that mistake. What was I doing?

What was I *thinking*? What the hell yyyyyyyyyyyyyyy
yyyyyyyyyyyyyyyyyyyyyyyyyyyyyyyyyyyyyyyyyyyyyyyyyyy
yyyyyyyyyyyyyyyyyyyyyyyyyyyyyyyyyyyyyyyyyyyyyyyyyyy

yyyyyyyyyyyyyyyyyyyyyyyyyyyyyyyyyyyyyyyyyyyyyyyyyyyyyyy yyyyyyyyyyyyyyyyyyyyyyyyy was going on?

"For that matter," said Simon, "what the hell is with all the 'y's'?"

"Oh," I said, looking, "I think the cat stepped on the keyboard."

"Pompous animals," Simon said.

"Yeah," I said. "You guys are right though. I'm *not* thinking clearly. Not at all. Oh, hang on a second, I think the traffic's moving."

I pulled up three feet and then put it back in park.

"Something must have happened back there," I said.

"In the strip joint?" Simon asked. "Or three feet behind us?"

"Strip joint. Zodar . . . Zodar must have done something. Messed with my head somehow. Got me thinking all weird."

"Duuuuuuude, I know *exactly* what you mean," Jimmy said. "I got some bad mescaline this one time? Oh man, you just don't know. Been *there*, done *that.*"

"I don't think he slipped me any acid Jimmy," I said.

"Whoa dude, you never know. They're pretty small."

"Be that as it may, I don't think Zodar relies on pharmaceuticals. No, he has a power, a presence, that we weren't made aware of. If he could affect my thinking that easily and that quickly, we're going to have to be very careful when we're around him next time."

"Hey," Jimmy said, "maybe we can make some brain shields out of aluminum foil."

"I don't think you have anything to worry about Jimmy," Simon said.

"Yeah, he'll be fine. But you and me Simon, we'll

have to be very careful indeed."

I gripped the wheel firmly with both hands and stared ahead with a renewed -and somewhat clearer -resolve. Head games. Huh. I should have suspected. No Russian animal worth his salt relies on brute force alone. Fool me once, shame on you. Fool me twice, . . . er . . . shame on you again, I guess. That's what my Mom used to tell me. That or something like it. Anyway, the point is, there'd be no fooling Dick Lassiter again. And if there was, it would be the moose's fault.

"Um, Dick?" Simon asked.

"Yeah?"

"We're still just kind of sitting here. Are we going to actually do something? In the next day or two I mean."

"Yeah," I said. "We are."

I shifted the Impala into drive, turned the wheel hard right, and gunned it. Some people may laugh at my choice in transportation, but I'll tell ya, here's where having a big old piece of full size Detroit iron really comes in handy. Just ask the owners of the half dozen Hondas' and Lexus' that I pushed out of my way and left dented, dripping, and smoking as I made it to the break down lane. My car suffered a scuff on the front bumper that I had to buff out later. I call that a win.

We blew down the shoulder faster than grandma running to the bathroom when her Ex-Lax kicks in. We had a moose to catch.

Chapter 29

Theme parks are scary at night. They're pretty creepy in the daytime too if you ask me, but at night they're invaded by shadows and an eerie quiet that makes the decor, so perpetually cheerful in the light of day, seem especially bizarre and threatening.

If you're not sure what I'm talking about, take a drive out into the country sometime, spend the night alone in abandoned farmhouse in an isolated part of the woods, and read Stephen King's "*IT*" by candlelight in one of the empty rooms on the second floor.

The feeling's close to that.

The tourists were gone for the day and the maintenance workers were the only ones in sight, sprucing and cleaning for tomorrow. That was pretty creepy too; kind of like in *West World* when they came out at night and cleaned up all of the dead robot cowboys? Except it wasn't quite the same since everyone on the maintenance crew here had headphones strapped to their heads and music cranked up so loud *we* could hear it. Somehow, knowing that they were all listening to Snoop Dogg or Justin Timberlake took the edge off a little and made them all seem not nearly so sinister as the *West World* guys.

I know that many people are quite frightened of tall black rappers and boy-band graduates, but luckily, we are not. (Tall *white* rappers however, are a completely different matter; a chance encounter with Vanilla Ice outside a KFC several years ago made Jimmy shit his pants on the spot and gave Simon & I anxiety attacks for weeks afterward).

We were overlooking the Magic Kingdom from a wooded hill on the Eastern side. Those of you who've been to the Magic Kingdom may be thinking something stupid right now, like "there is no wooded hill next to Disney on the Eastern side".

It always amazes me how tourists can come down for a couple days and suddenly think they know everything. So if you're one of those people, just let me say this: There is most *definitely* a wooded hill next to the Magic Kingdom, it's just very cleverly disguised as the sky, so you don't notice it unless you know it's there. You don't. I do. So shut up and hop on I-4, smart guy.

We were just finishing the final touches on our camouflage face paint. I glanced at my partners and made a mental note to hold training on proper camouflage techniques with both of them at some future date.

Jimmy had accidentally applied Sex Wax instead of camo, so although his face had a nice healthy glow and would provide good, non-skid footing should that be needed, it really didn't do much to hide him. Simon had actually done the face painting fairly well, and looked quite satisfied with himself, but the bright pink polo shirt he was wearing didn't exactly make him Mr. Invisible either.

As I picked up the binoculars and made another sweep of the park, Jimmy and Simon decided this would be a good time to argue about call signs.

"You were Red Leader One last time," said Jimmy.

"That's because I'm *always* Red Leader One," Simon replied. "You're Goldilocks."

"I don't want to be Goldilocks," Jimmy whined. "Goldilocks is a *girl* call sign."

"It is not," Simon assured.

"Oh yeah? Then *you* be Goldilocks."

"I would if I could, Jimmy," Simon said, " but I can't."

"Why?"

"Because I'm Red Leader One."

"That's not fair." Jimmy looked in my direction and decided it was time to appeal to a higher authority. "Dick, Simon says I can't be Red Leader – "

"Hey, hey, hey, with the call signs already," I said, holding up my hand. "*I* decide who's who."

"Well, okay," Jimmy said. "But he was Red Leader One last time."

"I'm *always* Red – "

"You," I said to Simon, "will be Maverick this time." I pointed to Jimmy. "And you will be Goose. You know, like *Top Gun*?"

Simon looked like he'd taken a slight demotion until I reminded him that Tom Cruise had been a "Maverick" too. He brightened up then. Jimmy didn't appear to be ecstatic about 'Goose' either, but hey, it was better than Goldilocks, so he didn't say anything. Even so, I decided to sweeten the deal for him a little.

"Hey, Jimmy," I said.

"Yeah?"

"You know who Goose's wife was, don't you?'

"No, who?"

"Meg Ryan."

"Yeah?" he said, suddenly perking up. "Really?"

"Yeah. Really."

"So Dick, are *you* going to be Red Leader One?" Simon asked.

"No," I said. "I'm Iceman."

"Whooooa, that's *cool*," Jimmy said. "Iceman. Sweet."

"Can I be Iceman next time?" Simon asked. "I call dibs."

"You can't call dibs yet," Jimmy shot back. "You can't call dibs until we're done with this mission. That's against the rules. In fact – new rule – if you call dibs before the end of a mission it actually counts as an *anti-dib*. So I don't even have to call dibs now because I'm already ahead of you."

"Oh yeah?" Simon said. "Well I'm going to do a pre-new rule retraction of my dib, so – "

"Shut up you two," I said. "I see him."

Zodar was moving in the shadows, building to building, staying out of sight as only a moose could. There was no sign of Portia; I imagined her gagged and tied up somewhere, frightened eyes darting left and right, struggling against her bonds, hoping against hope that she would live to see another day and not be partially submersed in an acid bath and then fed to sharks, or be shredded to bits by the Thunder Mountain Railroad and then have her remains dehydrated into commercial grade beef jerky to be sold for profit by certain less than reputable small town grocers, or possibly even . . . um . . . well, probably just those two things.

And she was probably somewhere high.

I kept my eye on Zodar, trying to gauge his moves, figure out his game. Up to this point he had just been *skulking*, staying out of sight from the random employees crisscrossing the park. And then suddenly, as he was moving from his hiding place behind a lovely topiary shaped like a duck towards the old abandoned *20,000 Leagues Under the Sea* ride, he disappeared completely.

I pulled the binoculars from my eyes, blinked, and then re-set them firmly against my face and looked again. He was gone. Vanished.

I swept the area back and forth, looking for a logical explanation, a clue, or maybe even some homeless guy that might have seen where he went and would cop him out for a dollar. Sometimes I get lucky that way, but not today. The only things around the spot I last saw him were some big fake rocks, a couple of benches, a trash can with towel racks hanging off the side, a face painting kiosk, and another one of those topiaries, this one not quite so lovely and shaped somewhat like a moose.

I turned to Jimmy and Simon, hoping that maybe they had caught something that I hadn't. Luckily, they had both been diverting all of their focus into not paying any attention at all, and were actually having a quiet conversation that they had decided to take off-line:

"You know that Goose dies, right?" said Simon in a hushed voice.

"Dude, that is so wrong," whispered Jimmy. "Why do you have to be like that?"

"Like what?" Simon replied, feigning innocence. "I'm just telling you the way it is. I thought you should know."

My partners. I almost wished bullets would start flying just so I could see if my theory that having them along statistically reduced my chances of being shot was actually correct.

Wait a minute.

I jerked the binoculars back up to my face.

The topiary! That wasn't a real tree, it was *Zodar*!

"Jimmy! Simon! Come on, were moving in!"

Normally, one would assume that giving orders in an excited yet clandestine manner would impart the feeling of urgency to those at which the communication was directed, especially in circumstances where your very survival demanded total concentration, nerves of steel, and split second timing.

Simon and Jimmy obviously felt that the current situation was clearly not normal at all, was in fact devoid of any danger whatsoever, and thus felt no need to get overly worked up about it. However, I will give credit where credit is due; they did at least stop their conversation for a moment.

"Who us?" they chimed in unison, looking at me with blank faces.

"Yes! He's right there! We can take him, but we've got to move now!"

Simon finally got it. "Roger that Iceman," he said, "Red Lead – I mean, *Maverick* – online and standing by."

"Oh, okay," Jimmy said, "Goose is ready. I'm Goose."

"Roger Goose," said Simon, "reading you five by five."

"What?" Jimmy said,

"I said, I'm reading you – "

"*Will you guys knock it off!*" I yelled.

A silence descended so complete that for a moment I thought I'd killed them both. Jimmy & Simon stared at me with eyes wide and mouths shut.

"Do we have hedge clippers?" I asked Simon finally.

"Yes," he said. "Well, you and I do anyway. I brought safety scissors for Jimmy."

"Good thinking. Let's break 'em out then. Lock and load," I said. I took my feet and stood tall, staring down the hillside with a defiant gaze.

"It's time to do some landscaping."

Chapter 30

Had conditions been different, the three of us would have crept with all due stealth down the side of the hill, however, the magic of Disney doesn't necessarily lend itself well to covert operations. To be more specific, three men creeping down the side of a hill that was painted to look like the sky has a tendency to really make those three men stand out, and in a really weird way.

So we just ran down and screamed our asses off.

"Zodar! Shape Shifter! We're coming for you!"

"Give it up G! I ain't holding the down!"

"I'm Goose! I'm Goose!"

The sight of three crazed men armed with hedge clippers and safety scissors storming the gate effectively reminded the night crew that they all worked for minimum wage and that, with no other allegiance to the park of any significance, they were not honor bound to stand and protect their ground. It should be noted that whether or not these thoughts consciously went through any of their minds as they scattered like roaches is still a topic of much debate in many academic circles.

Things were going quite well until we came to the fence. In the classic theme park tradition of disguising things to look like something other than what they actually are, the fence was cleverly designed to bear a striking resemblance to the type of fence that might be found at someplace other than a theme park. By the look of it, we assumed that it fell into the category of fences that "aren't too strong and will fall if hit with any reasonable amount of force."

In this we miscalculated to some degree.

I found out much later that a crew of maintenance workers who witnessed the event from one of the towers of Cinderella's Castle gave us a combined score of 9.4 for what they termed our "Triple-Thud". The total would have been higher, however, a low score given by the lone French janitor pulled it down, thus arousing much suspicion in the process since one of Simon's twice removed cousins is Canadian.

After a moment of stunned bird watching & stargazing, I shook off the pain and launched myself over the top of the fence, which achieved the objective of getting me to the other side much better than my first attempt. Jimmy, no stranger to pain himself and a regular frequent flyer when it came to colliding with wooden objects (like fishing pier foundations), followed a moment later and appeared relatively unfazed. Or, to be more precise, appeared no more fazed than usual.

The appearance of Simon, however, was less sudden than I would have preferred.

"Simon!" I yelled. "Come on!"

His continued lack of attendance on the business side of the fence was enjoying an apparently prolonged relationship with a rather annoying silence. Not being one to jump to conclusions, I resisted the urge to make any knee jerk assumptions, such as labeling Simon a coward of the type who would use this fence incident as an excuse to bail out on the team just when we needed him the most. Instead – and keeping my emotions in check just as I had been taught in my 12-Step anger management program – I quickly but calmly explored a few of the other possible scenarios for Simon's absence:

a) he was dead
b) he thought he was dead and didn't want to confuse
   things by speaking
c) he had booked an ill-timed vacation to Central
   America and was now being held at gunpoint by
   Panamanian rebels in a small warehouse near the
   Columbian border (there's Columbia again; go
   figure)
d) he had found Portia and was trying to score
e) he had fallen into a den of boa constrictors and was
   fighting for his life with one that had wrapped
   itself around his neck
f) he had –

"Dick," came the pitiful wail from the far side of the fence, "I'm hurt."

"Simon!" I yelled, "Get over here! We're right in the middle of an assault. This is no time to be goofing around."

"But my leg hurts, Dick. My shin. I hurt it bad. I can't make it. You guys go on without me."

Coward it was. Always stick with your gut.

"Your shin hurts?" I said.

"Yeah, it hurts bad. Like I said, I don't think I'm going to make it. You guys go on without – "

"Is it bleeding?"

Pause. "What?"

"I said, is it bleeding?"

"Um . . . well, no, but – "

"Is it broken?"

"Broken?"

"Yeah, broken. Is it broken?"

"Um . . . wait a minute," he said. Then, a few moments later, "Well, I don't think it's broken *per se*, but I think there's a good possibility that it might be slightly dislocated."

"Really. You're telling me you dislocated your shin."

"Yeah, or sprained it or something. Hey, I'm not a doctor, but it's a mess alright, that's for sure. Listen, I don't want slow you guys down. Just go, leave me here. I'll make it back on my own. Somehow."

"Simon?" I said.

"Yeah, Dick?"

"You got five seconds to get over that fence, and three of 'em are already gone."

In less time than it takes to say "Trix are for kids", Simon landed smartly on his feet next to me.

"Dislocated, huh?" I said.

"Yeah, well," he said sheepishly, "Prompt first aid, you know? And I'm a pretty quick healer anyway."

"Good thing, because when we're done with all of this I'm gonna beat the shit out of you. It'll hurt me to do that, of course, but I'll take comfort in knowing that you bounce back quickly."

"Yeah, um, . . . hey, oh man, does my head hurt! I must've really knocked myself senseless there. What just happened? remember hitting the fence, and now I'm standing next to you. How did I get here? What happened in between? I must've had a concussion or something. I usually start talking nonsense when that happens. Was I talking nonsense? Boy, I must've really been out of it just now. What could I possibly have said? I have no idea.

Dick, did you happen to hear anything – ”

"Simon, *shut up* and just follow me, okay?”

"Gotcha, Iceman.”

"And wake up Jimmy, will you?”

"Will do.”

Back to full strength and luckily having lost only a few moments to the entire fence incident, we resumed our charge, intent on a kill.

Jimmy had found a bucket of water somewhere and, screaming "Freeze, assmoose!", promptly threw the entire contents on the topiary, drenching it's delicate, painstakingly sculpted branches.

An instant later, Simon and I hit it at full steam, our hedge clippers ripping into the dripping foliage with reckless abandon. Leaves and branches flew in all directions, and in a matter of seconds, nothing remained but a ragged stump amid a sea of horticultural carnage.

No way was Zodar shape shifting out of this mess. And if he did, it would have to be as a bunch of tiny little Zodars, and we would have just stomped the hell out of them.

Panting, dripping wet, and looking like we had survived a spinach explosion, Simon and I threw our clippers to the ground. Not breathing heavily, completely dry, and looking otherwise none the worse for wear, Jimmy threw down the bucket. His unused safety scissors remained stuck in his belt.

"Say, Jimmy,” I said, hands on my knees.

"Yeah?” he replied.

"What,” I said, still trying to catch my breath, "what was the deal . . . with the bucket?”

"The bucket?” he said. "It was full of water.”

"I *know* it was full of water. But why did you throw it at Zodar?"

"Well, I found it and got an idea. I figured I'd just get him soaking wet, and then the water would freeze, and then he'd be trapped. Frozen solid."

Simon and I looked at each other a moment. He either had no clue what Jimmy was talking about either or was telling the truth about his head injury.

"Jimmy," I said, "how was he going to freeze? It's 87 degrees."

"Did you just mean to make a rhyme, Dick?" Simon asked. "Because you just did."

"*SHUT UP* Simon!" I yelled.

"Okay."

I turned back to Jimmy, letting my original question hang in the air. He was obviously thinking about it.

"Oh," he said finally. "water won't freeze if it's hot, will it?"

"No, Jimmy. It won't," I said.

"Whoa. That would explain a lot. I was wondering why he just kept dripping." The hurt look on his face inspired me to take pity.

"It's okay, Jimmy. It's okay. We got him. And if nothing else, I'm sure the bucket of water confused the hell out of him."

"You think?" he said, brightening up.

"I think."

The finality of any dangerous, difficult mission brings about a relieved euphoria, and we were all feeling it. Boyish grins and a shared giddiness at our own survival soon turned into chuckles and laughter, even as we stood among the chaos and devastation of the vegetation.

Simon almost made another rhyming comment just then, but saw the look in my eye and thought better of it. No need to ruin the moment.

"Alright men," I said. "Looks like we're going to have to clean up this mess ourselves. Wouldn't want any small children to have to see this in the morning."

Simon and Jimmy exchanged knowing looks and nodded.

"Jimmy," I continued, "get that broom over there and start sweeping this up into a pile. Simon, why don't you bring that trashcan over here and we'll start scooping this stuff into it."

"Uh, Dick?" Simon asked.

"What now?" I replied.

"What trashcan?"

"The trashcan right over th – "

I stopped. The trashcan was gone.

An uneasy feeling suddenly crept up my spine. There *had* been a trashcan, I was sure of it. I looked back a couple of pages to Chapter 29 just to make sure I remembered correctly. Yup, there it was alright, a trashcan with towel racks hanging off the sides. But where was it now? Where had it gone?

And then it hit me like a pillowcase full of canned corn.

"Those weren't towel racks! Those were *antlers*!" I yelled. "He's the trashcan! Zodar's disguised as the trashcan!"

"You know," said Simon, "I was going to ask you about that. I mean, who puts towel racks on a trashcan anyway? Seemed kind of strange to me. In hindsight, I probably should have mentioned it."

"Dude, you mean he's still alive?" Jimmy said.

"Come on, quick," I said, "look for the trashcan! Where did it go?"

We spread out, looking frantically in all directions. Seconds passed, and I feared we had lost him completely, when Jimmy suddenly yelled out.

"Dudes! There he is!" he said, pointing. "Check him out! That trashcan is *cruisin'*."

"After him!" I yelled.

We broke out in a full sprint after our clever quarry, chasing him toward Tomorrowland.

Somewhere in the distance, a clock struck midnight.

Chapter 31

Publisher's Note: Chapter 31 consists of a prolonged chase sequence which, while several pages in length and filled with a considerable amount of pursuit and an abundance of almost catching, is neither overly humorous nor particularly interesting. As such, the publishers have deleted this chapter in its entirety as a preventive effort to preclude the possibility of the reader losing any further interest in the story and not finishing it at all. Suffice to say that by the end of Chapter 31, all concerned have traversed extended distances, are extremely winded, and have wound up at the entrance to Space Mountain.

We thank you for your patience and understanding. Please also visit our website to view our entire line of other exciting and better written publications. We now return you to the story.

Chapter 32

"Did you see what just happened?" I said.

We were all extremely winded and dripping with sweat. Zodar had just disappeared into the darkened entrance of Space Mountain and were catching our breath before heading in after him. I'm in pretty good shape for someone who smokes two packs a day, routinely skips breakfast & lunch, and doesn't exercise at all, but I'll be the first to admit that even I was feeling it. We had traversed quite a bit of distance in the past hour.

"See what?" Simon said.

"Chapter 31," I said.

"Yeah? What about it?"

"They took it out."

"*What?* It's missing?" Simon exclaimed. "Somebody took it?"

"No," I replied, "they didn't take it. They *deleted* it."

"*Who* deleted it?"

"Publisher."

"You're kidding me. What the hell for?"

"Said it wasn't exciting. Didn't want to bore anybody."

"That's *bullshit*. You mean I just did all that running around for *nothing*?"

"We were *all* running, Simon."

"Okay, okay. 'Go team' and all that. You mean *we* just did all that running around for nothing?"

"Looks like it."

"You've *got* to be kidding me. Boring? *That* was

boring? That made Steve McQueen's car chase in *Bullitt* look like a game of lawn bowling."

"Yeah," I said. "It is somewhat of an artistic dissatisfier."

"*Unbelievable* is what it is. Absolutely unbelievable. See, this is what I was telling you, Dick. This kind of stuff doesn't happen in a – "

"Hey," Jimmy interrupted, "what happened to the chase scene?"

"Nevermind, Jimmy," I said. "It doesn't matter. Come on guys. We still have work to do."

"Well, I'll be damned if I'm running my ass off anymore trying to do it, that's for sure," Simon said.

I shook my head. "I don't think we have to. Look."

A line of crimson dots on the ground, accentuated periodically with a red smear, led a wavy trail into the darkness of Space Mountain. Zodar was bleeding. Somehow, in all the mayhem of the exciting chase that you didn't get to read about, Zodar had been hurt. If that was true, he wouldn't be so hard to catch now.

"He won't be so hard to catch now," Simon said.

"Nope. Not if he's hurt," Jimmy added.

"Hey, are you two eavesdropping on my thoughts again?" I asked sharply.

"What?" Simon said, his eyes opening in alarm. "No way. Not me. Swear to God, I thought that up all by myself. I mean, you've got to admit, it's a pretty obvious statement, right?"

"Yeah," chimed Jimmy, "pretty obvious."

I glared at them for a couple seconds, letting them squirm in the silence. Then I just let it go. I didn't believe them, of course, but I was too tired to make an issue out of it. Besides, I felt we all would need what strength we had left. Because somewhere up the dark corridor in front of us was a wounded animal.

And he was cornered.

The darkness thickened as we proceeded silently up the ramp into the tunnel, but not enough to keep me from noticing that our threesome had lost some weight by the time we were about 100 feet in. To be more exact, Simon wasn't with us. But I knew where he was.

I turned around and, sure enough, there was his silhouetted frame standing back at the entrance to the tunnel. Either by good vision or better guessing, he knew that I saw him.

"Hey, Dick," he said, "I better stay back here in case he slips past you and tries to sneak out."

What a coward. But by this time I was tired of trying to carry him along, and I couldn't afford to waste any more time. Zodar was injured, and that would slow him down some, but he wasn't in a coma. If I gave him time to think, he would. And a moose that has time to think is a moose that can figure out a way to escape. I had let him slip past me back at the strip joint and no way was I going to let that happen again.

I suddenly realized that I had forgotten all about Portia and I briefly wondered where the hell she had wound up. Oh well. Not my problem anymore. The world had grown cold again.

"Good idea," I yelled back to Simon. I turned and started back up the ramp. "Come on, Jimmy. Let's finish this thing."

"This moose is so toast," he said.

I liked the resolve in his voice.

I pulled out my gun and we started walking.

If the publishers thought that our chase of Zodar through Tomorrowland was too long, I wasn't going to bother them with the details of my and Jimmy's descent into the bowels of Space Mountain. Holy shit. Every time you thought you were close to the end there was another corner, or a switch-back, or an entry into a whole new room. The chains, turnstiles, and human cattle chutes went on forever. No wonder tourists came down to stay for a whole week. It takes half a day just to walk from the "entrance" of a ride to where the ride actually was. And there wasn't anybody in front of us either.

Well, that wasn't entirely true.

The drops of blood on the floor were now barely visible in the darkness, but I could still see enough to tell that Zodar was limping badly from the pattern they made. We had covered a good 2, maybe three miles, and I could no longer hear Simon's brave shouts of encouragement as he boldly guarded the entrance far away from any real danger. But I could hear something else now that I hadn't been able to hear before over the din of Simon's prattle: heavy, labored breathing.

"Jimmy," I whispered, "do you hear that?"

"What?" he replied, in a voice that was probably normal in volume but under the circumstances sounded loud enough to hail a soldier 100 yards away in the midst of a fierce battle.

"*Shhhhhh!*" I whispered urgently, "you'll give us away! We're getting real close now."

"It's alright, Dick," came a weary voice out of the darkness ahead. "I know you're there."

"Oh yeah?" replied Jimmy back to the darkness.

"Well, we knew that you knew we were here. How about that?" Jimmy then turned to me and, to make sure I was up to date on the conversation, whispered, "I told him that we knew that he knew we were here."

"Nice job, Jimmy," I said.

"No problem, dude. I'm here for you."

Nice to know I had that going for me. I think. I could almost see Jimmy's conspiratorial wink, and, fearing a surfer hug and the subsequent male bonding that would follow, I did what any red-blooded American male would do. I changed the subject.

"Zodar," I called out, "it's over. We know everything. There's nothing left to keep fighting for. Let's end this peacefully."

"Yeah," said Jimmy, "so put your hooves up and come on out."

Maybe not the exact choice of words I would have used, but at least he was in the ball park. A little further out in center field than I would have liked, but in the same park no less.

The sound of low laughter. Then, "I'm afraid, gentlemen, that if I put my hooves up, I wouldn't be *able* to come out. That would put us in quite the stalemate, would it not?"

"Oh, okay," said Jimmy. "Just forget that part then. But everything that Dick said still goes."

"Thanks, Jimmy," I said. "I'll take it from here."

"Okay."

I began a conversation with Zodar to keep him distracted while I quietly started moving forward again in the darkness. Jimmy followed dutifully.

"Zodar," I said, "I know what you're going through."

"Do you now?"

"Absolutely. The nation that created you – and that you loyally served – has crumbled and turned its back on you. You've been maligned in world public opinion because of what Rok and Stinky Pete did. There was probably something pretty bad that happened in your childhood. And the woman you loved has tossed you aside like an old shoe."

"What woman?"

"Um . . . Portia?"

"No idea who you're talking about."

"Fair enough. Scratch the broken heart. But if that's truly the case, then let me go back and elaborate a little more on the childhood trauma thing, okay?"

"No deal."

Damn. I *had* to keep him talking. We were getting close. I could *feel* it. I had to keep him talking & distracted so I could sneak up and put a bullet in him.

"Okay then," I said. "But I don't understand something."

"And what is that?"

"What? Well, nothing that you can help me with really. In fact, it doesn't have anything to do with you at all, just something to do with mimes that's had me puzzled for a long – oh, wait. Yeah, you know, there *is* something you might be able to answer for me. Just thought of it. Why, Zodar? Why?"

"I thought a man of your caliber would have figured that out already, Lassiter."

"Hey dude," Jimmy said to me, "he just called you by your last name. That's cool."

"Really?" I replied. "Is ignoring people cool too?"

"Oh yeah. Very."

"Then watch this." I turned my attention back to the moose.

"You've been wronged Zodar. No debate there. But did you really think that world domination would somehow make it all better? You're smarter than that. A moose like you, with your talents, you could have done anything you wanted. You could have had it all."

"That *was* my general intention."

"Oh yeah. Good point. I guess that was a pretty stupid line of argument I was using just now, wasn't it?"

"Quite."

"Yeah, well. But is that what all of this was for? Revenge?"

"You really *don't* understand, do you Lassiter? No, you couldn't."

"So why don't you try explaining it to me."

"Why should I? So you can keep me talking & distracted while you sneak up and put a bullet in me?"

Damn, this guy was *good*. But if I was going to take him down, I was going to have to be better. Up ahead I could see what appeared to be the actual, final, no shit end of the tunnel. All I needed was a few more seconds. I called his bluff.

"You know I'm going to do that anyway, Zodar."

"I know that you're going to *try*."

"Alright, Zodar. Enough. No more word games. Talk or don't talk. Doesn't matter much to me. But just on the off chance that I'm the one who winds up walking out of here, wouldn't you like at least one person to understand?"

There was a few moments of tense silence as my

words struck home.

"You're right," Zodar said finally. "Regardless of how this turns out, you at least should know."

I was only 20 feet from where the tunnel ended. Beyond that was a warm glow of light coming from what appeared to be a large room that the tunnel fed into. I couldn't tell any more than that, but I knew Zodar was in there. I moved silently, slowly, tight against the wall.

"All of my life," Zodar said, "I am raised Soviet. All of my memories, everything I did, everything I was taught, was for the sake of the State. Loyalty. Honor. Duty. Sacrifice. Always for the betterment of the State. I never knew my mother and my father, if I even had a mother and father."

"Boy," I whispered to Jimmy, "did I have that childhood thing pegged or what?"

"Nailed it, dude," he whispered back.

"But I didn't mind," Zodar continued. "I had a purpose. I could make a difference, and help the people of my country. So I trained, I studied, and I never lost faith in what I was doing or who I was doing it for. It wasn't about me, after all. It was about the Motherland."

"This is getting kind of political, don't you think?" Jimmy whispered.

"Yeah. I know it's boring, but just hang in there, I think he's almost done," I answered quietly, still moving towards the corner.

"And then, suddenly, the Cold War was over," Zodar said. "I confess, I never saw it coming. And I never thought my mighty Soviet Union would collapse. And I never thought that, just as quickly, my country wouldn't need me anymore."

"Yeah," I called out. "I can see why you might be pissed at them. But we knew *that* part. We're just trying to figure out why you're over here screwing around with us."

"Them?" Zodar said sharply, "I'm not angry at *them*, I'm angry at *you*."

"Um, say what?"

"If it wasn't for *you*, the Cold War wouldn't have ended, the Soviet Union would still exist, and I would be a hero in my homeland!"

"Well, technically I didn't have anything to do with that."

"But your country did!"

"Oh yeah," I said, "Now that you mention it, I remember reading that part in your note. But hey, in that note you also said you were angry at your *own* country too. In fact, that was the *first* thing you mentioned, the whole 'mad at those who created you' thing."

"I lied. I am a spy, after all. It's what I do."

"Good point."

We had reached the end of the tunnel. I raised my gun chest high and nodded at Jimmy. Time to play. I jumped out of the tunnel into the dimly lit room. Jimmy landed next to me an instant later.

Time slowed down.

In the first half-second, my brain had time to register that the room was huge, and filled with a literal maze of those metal people railing thingies. The walls and ceilings were decorated with planets & stars, and large television monitors hung at intervals along the walls. On the far end was an open area where I could see a futuristic roller coaster sitting lifeless on the tracks. And just in front of the coaster was Zodar, wounded & weary, looking back at me.

In the second half-second, my brain had time to register numerous blinding flashes of light and a corresponding number of very loud '*Blams*'.

Full second #2 of our arrival into the room entered with both Jimmy and I eating carpet as the bullets that were fired at us back in the second half-second of the first second whizzed over our heads.

Time sped back up to normal. Thank God.

As the shooting stopped we lay cringed on the floor, while bits & pieces of broken plastic and drywall bounced on the floor around us.

Suddenly, Jimmy jumped to his feet.

"That's six shots Zodar!" he yelled. "You're out of bullets!"

Blam! Blam! Blam! Blam! Blam! Blam! Blam!

Jimmy decided to rejoin me on the floor. A good career move all around.

"Dude," he said, eyes like saucers, "I think he's got an automatic."

"No shit?" I said.

"Either that or he can reload really, *really,* fast."

"Thanks for that valuable input, Jimmy. I appreciate it."

"No problem."

It's always a little embarrassing to find yourself cowering on the floor under a hail of gunfire, especially after you've spent so much time and effort sneaking up on someone with the intent of blowing them full of holes.

Sure, in hindsight, maybe I had lost a little too much of the element of surprise by holding a conversation during the whole "sneaking up" process, but I had consciously given that up, believing that my "jumping into the middle of a big open space in front of a dangerous, armed villain with an entrenched defensive position" strategy would give me the edge I needed to take him down.

Once again, I had underestimated my foe, and for the first time, slivers of self-doubt started to wiggle into my mind. Could I actually defeat this menace, or was Zodar simply too tough? Could it be that he was just better than me? Smarter than me? Had I finally met my match?

Then a new thought hit me: Hey, I had a gun too.

Chapter 33

Sun Tzu's *"The Art of War"* is a well-known, time honored classic that, to this day, is often praised for its wise, philosophical perspective on armed combat. Being in my line of work, it should then come as no surprise to you that there was a time when I once studied this work in great detail.

Okay, okay; so I skimmed through it once during a commercial break while I was watching *Everybody Loves Raymond*, it still makes me somewhat of an authority, and as such, I feel righteously empowered to tell you that most of it's just a bunch of crap.

There was, however, something in there about "knowing your enemy" that made at least a little bit of sense to me, and, not being one to waste good insight, regardless of where it might have come from, I took the liberty to modify that particular bit of wisdom and include it into my own personal "Guidelines of Warfare", the entire text of which is printed below:

1) Know where your enemy is
2) Shoot at him a lot

While never having received quite the critical media acclaim as other publications dealing with the same subject matter, many laymen have embraced my philosophy for its simplicity, no-nonsense approach, and ease of implementation.

As proof of my own confidence in this strategy, you

should be aware that at this point, I jumped to my feet, aimed my gun in the direction of Zodar, and started scratching my trigger finger.

BLAM! BLAM! BLAM! BLAM! BLAM! BLAM! BLAM! BLAM! BLAM! BLAM! BLAM! BLAM! BLAM! BLAM! BLAM!

I paused and glared out through the smoke – steel eyed, adrenaline pumping – watching for any movement. I wasn't sure if I'd hit him or not, but I was pretty certain that I'd at least made a valid point to him regarding my current mood. Then, just to make sure he didn't think I was kidding, I let go a few more.

BLAM! BLAM! BLAM! BLAM! BLAM! BLAM! BLAM! BLAM! BLAM!

Put that in your pipe and smoke it, moose. I stopped again and gave him time to chew on it a while.

"I see you've changed weapons on me," Zodar said from somewhere on the far side of the room. "You're carrying an automatic now too."

"No, I'm not. I just reload really, *really*, fast."

There was a moment of hesitation before his reply, and when it finally came, it came with a hint of uncertainty.

"I . . . I guess you do at that," he said.

He was rattled. I could feel it. And about time, too. Up until now, Zodar had been playing with a stacked deck, showing trump after trump. But I'd finally found a card that he couldn't match; when it came to pulling a trigger, *nobody* was faster than Dick Lassiter. Now if I could just get a good look at his furry ass, I'd square my sights and end this once and for all.

I risked a quick glance down at my feet. Jimmy was as horizontal as a man can get, either still cowering or sound asleep, I couldn't tell. I gave him a nudge with my foot and, moments later, he was up by my side.

"Time to button him up," I said.

My gun still raised, we started moving slowly toward the other side of room. Normally, we would have started moving quickly toward the other side of the room, but we had to stop every two feet to climb over those damn metal rails. But it was either that or walk between the rails and look like a couple of idiots zigzagging back and forth.

We were halfway there, and I was straddled over another railing, when I saw a soda can skitter across the floor towards the roller coaster. A soda can with big old honkin' antlers that is. Sorry Zodar, not this time. I wasn't falling for that again.

I took a bead on him, but just as I pulled the trigger, my foot slipped off the metal bar where some punk kid had spilled ice cream on it or something. Luckily, I only fell about six inches, at which point my fall was broken as the railing came into firm contact with my crotch.

BLAM!

What should have been the period at the end of the sentence instead slammed harmlessly into the floor several feet behind the scrambling can, sending chips of concrete screaming into the far wall.

And speaking of screaming, I was doing a little of that myself as I stared at the ceiling and admired a few new constellations that I hadn't noticed before. Jimmy had seen what happened and reacted accordingly.

"Duuuuuude!" he said, "Oh *man*, that had to hurt."

In a typical male sympathy reaction, he grabbed his own crotch with both hands and – half-staggering, half-hopping – limped around in circles, sharing my pain.

"Ouch! Ouch! Ouch! Oh dude, you're hatin' it. Ohhhhh, man, *that's* gonna leave a mark."

I grit my teeth and focused all of my energy in an attempt to clear my head. After what seemed like an eternity, a few of the stars at last flickered and went out. Then, in the lowest tone of voice I could muster, I said, "Jimmy, help me down."

"Right. Help you down," he said.

Very slowly – and very carefully – Jimmy helped me raise my leg over the bar until I was once again standing gingerly on terra firma with both feet. I took a few tentative steps to see how my motor skills were working. Definitely not 100%, but I'd recover. As the last of the fog lifted from my mind, I became aware of an unusual mechanical hum and, seconds later, of lights flashing.

"Quick, Jimmy!" I yelled in a voice that was still a little high in tone, "He's getting away!"

With no hope of jumping the rails in my present condition, we ran/hobbled along the forced pathway as fast as we could toward the roller coaster, now alive and starting to move. Zodar was in the front car, back in full moose form. He was smiling at us as he raised his automatic.

Jimmy and I were sitting ducks. Hell, we probably

even *looked* a little like ducks, moving back and forth across the room as we maneuvered through the human cattle chutes. Didn't matter though.

I was mad, and I wasn't thinking about taking cover now. I was thinking about where I could find a good taxidermist.

"I'm sorry it has to end this way, Lassiter," Zodar said smugly. "Unlike my former country, I will not fold under the pressure of a capitalist regime that exists solely to oppress the – "

Fortunately for us, at that moment the front car of the roller coaster, with Dr. Pontification still firmly in its grasp, disappeared from view on its way into the darkness of Space Mountain.

Hey, you snooze, you lose. He had his shot.

Unfortunately for us, the remaining cars of the coaster were following the first in a smart, orderly fashion.

"Hurry, Jimmy!" I urged. "We've got to get on that coaster!"

Finally, mercifully, we rounded the last bend of the rails and came into the clear. Most of the roller coaster was gone from view now, and the few cars that remained were rapidly disappearing as they picked up speed.

Fighting pain, nausea, and fatigue, we ran as fast as we could across the loading platform and jumped into the very last car just as it slid behind the wall.

We crumpled to the floor and were enveloped by darkness.

Chapter 34

We were in another tunnel, colored lights flashing from front to back, giving the illusion of speed. Jimmy was staring at them as if in a trance.

"Wow," he said. "Check out the lights, dude. That's trippin'."

The only trip I was taking was the one headed straight to Mooseville.

I got up on my knees, leveled my gun, and squeezed off a few shots, not really looking to hit anything, but just to make my presence known. In the process, the wind blew my fedora off my head, momentarily confusing me and, of course, leaving me hatless.

Zodar picked up quickly on the clue and popped a couple of caps back at me to let me know he cared.

Blam! Blam!
BLAM! BLAM!
Blam! Blam! Blam!
BLAM!
Blam! Blam!
BLAM! BLAM! BLAM! BLAM!

And so it went for a few moments as Zodar and I locked horns in mortal combat, the sounds of gunfire punctuated only by the occasional "Whoa", "Dude", and "Trippin' man" uttered by Jimmy as he continued his fascinated observance of the colored lights and twinkling stars as we barreled through the universe. Up and down, a light swerve left, a hard jig right, the coaster paid us no mind as it went about its merry way, never knowing the havoc it was playing on our marksmanship.

"Zodar!" I yelled. "Enough!"

Blam! Blam! Blam! he answered.

"Oh yeah?" I screamed.

BLAM! BLAM! BLAM! BLAM! click, click, click, click.

"Uh-oh," I said, dropping back down in the seat. "Jimmy, I'm out of bullets."

"Dude, look!" Jimmy said, pointing. "There's the Big Dipper! That is soooo cool!"

"Jimmy, will you knock it off? Were in some amount of shit here, okay? I'm out of ammo. Do you understand? I. Have. No. Bullets."

Ever cool under even the most dire circumstances, Jimmy continued not to pay any attention to a thing I was saying. He was enthralled with the ride.

"Look! Look!" he said, "There's Saturn! That's my planet dude!"

Suddenly, with years of fluid surfing agility and a speed that belied his normal laid back persona, Jimmy pushed himself up and hopped up on the back of the car. It happened so fast, he was up before I could lay a hand on him.

"WHOOO! Yeah, dog!" he yelled into the darkness. "Check me out, I'm space surfing, dude!"

"Jimmy!" I yelled, "Get down from there before – "

KLANG!

" – you hit your head on something."

Jimmy disappeared off of the back of the car and into the darkness as if by magic. And to my serious dismay, the coaster was now slowing down as it neared completion of its interstellar journey. We were pulling back into the station, and the combination of much better lighting & less motion coupled with my untimely lack of ammunition was sure to cause a problem or two in the survivability department.

The coaster was pulling to a stop, and Zodar was peering at me from the front car. No stranger to the obvious, he quickly noticed the absence of great quantities of lead flying in his direction and he rose higher, a wicked grin spreading across his face.

"I have you now," he said, raising his gun.

Not quite.

With no other viable options (I mean, really, like what, trying to run away with a sore crotch through all of those damn metal railings?) I reared back and threw my now useless gun at the big red button on the control panel of the operating station. The revolver hit it square on, and, with a jolt, the coaster started off again. I ducked down into my seat and felt the temporary safety of the darkness wash over me as we entered the tunnel again.

I lay there, staring up at the lights, and for a moment understood the fascination that they'd held for Jimmy as I awaited the inevitable. I had bought a momentary reprieve, but in just a few minutes we would again complete our journey and pull back into the station. That would be it. I had nothing else to throw at the big red button.

As the seconds ticked by, I contemplated my fate with a calm resolve. I remembered the white cyanide capsule in my pocket, and considered whether I should steal Zodar's thunder by taking myself out, rather than giving him the satisfaction of doing it himself. Somehow, the fact that I'd be dead either way took most of the fun out of it, so in the end, it didn't really matter to me.

Meanwhile, the coaster continued to make it's mindless way through the universe again, oblivious to everything else except forging ahead on it's well known course through the planets. Up and down we went. A light swerve left. A hard jig right.

I had an idea.

"Zodar!" I yelled out. "Can I ask you a question?"

"What for? A last request of a doomed man, perhaps?" he laughed.

"Might say that. Not a request though. Just a question."

"What is it?" came the reply.

"Are you, like, you know . . . a *girl* moose?"

"Excuse me?"

"You know, a girl moose. A smoothie. A Moosella."

"*WHAT?*"

"Yeah, well, I normally wouldn't ask, you know? Good etiquette and all that. It's just that, you know, you're really kind of a puss when you get right down to it."

"What . . .who do you . . . how *dare* you!"

"Struck a nerve, huh? Yeah, well, truth hurts I guess."

There was a moment of silence and then I heard him utter a menacing growl. I didn't think mooses could do that – growl, I mean – but apparently they can when they're really mad.

"I'm going to *enjoy* killing you, Lassiter," he said finally, without a drip of humor in his voice.

Boy, was he steamed. Good thing that's what I was hoping for. Now to really turn the screws.

"Hey, that's great and all, but try to hold it down up there for now, okay? I'm going to rest a while before you kill me and I really don't feel like listening to you flap your jowls like some bitch, alright? I'd appreciate it."

"I've got a good mind to come back there and kill you right now," he said.

"Yeah, right. Like *that'll* happen."

"I will. I mean it."

"Whatever you say Big Z. But I gotta tell you, I'm not exactly shaking in my shoes here, know what I mean?"

"Alright. That's it. You die now!"

I sat up in my seat and calmly watched as Zodar, furious, climbed out of the front car and started working his way back to me, steam shooting from his flared nostrils as he moved from car to car.

"Hey, you be careful there, okay?" I called out in a friendly voice.

"You should be worrying more about yourself, Lassiter. In a few moments you're going to be *extremely* dead."

"Nah. I'm not going to waste time worrying. Know why? Care to hazard a guess?"

"Do tell," he said, now halfway back to me and focusing so much attention to his footing that he didn't even notice the Big Dipper whizzing by.

"Because you can't kill me."

"Oh, really? And why is that?"

"Because I'm nothing. Understand? *Nothing.* Tough to kill that. I don't even exist. And not to upset you, but neither do you for that matter."

"What kind of nonsense – "

"Exist, I mean. You're nothing too."

"I'll show you who – "

"Nothing, you hear?"

"I'm – "

"*Nothing,*" I finished for him. "You are a figment of the imagination."

"I am *not!*" he screamed as he mounted the car directly in front of me. He rose to his full height and aimed the barrel of his gun directly into my face. "I am not *nothing!*"

Saturn flashed by behind his head.

"I am Zodar the Spy Moose!" he roared, "And you will *FEEL MY WRATH!*"

"Yeah? Well, I'm Dick Lassiter. And you want to talk about feeling something? Check this shit out."

KLANG!

In a blur of hooves, antlers, and fur, the spy moose that was Zodar raced over my head, and was gone. I breathed out a huge sigh of relief, and sat back as the coaster slowed down and pulled back into the station. With a slight jolt, it came to a stop.

I took out a cigarette, lit it, and pulled deep, grateful that there wasn't anyone around for a change to tell me to put it out. I just sat there a while, taking a few minutes to decompress. Felt the tension start to slowly ease from my muscles as I considered all that had happened. It was done.

I glanced up, and for the first time I noticed the sign over the coaster tunnel, a familiar warning that, as ludicrous as it sounds, can be found on roller coasters across America:

DO NOT STAND UP

Good advice.

Chapter 35

I was dozing in my chair, hat pulled down over my brow, feet up on the desk, when I heard the knock. I tilted my head and looked at the door.

"Enter," I said.

Jimmy and Simon bounded in and plopped down in the chairs in front of my desk. They had spent the last week hanging out together, getting drunk, playing video games, and patronizing strip joints under the pretense of searching for Portia, who we never did find, by the way. I was happy for them. Their relationship had come a long way since the beginning of this case.

Jimmy still had a big bandage on his forehead, but was otherwise in good repair. Simon, well, there wasn't anything wrong with Simon. At least nothing a good swift kick in the butt wouldn't cure.

I could tell by the look in their eyes what this was about.

"Heading back?" I said.

"Yeah, I think it's about time," Simon replied. "Pricilla keeps calling me on my cell. I think she's getting suspicious that I'm just goofing off. Wants me to come home. Put on my suit and go to the office and start working again and all that. I guess I probably should."

"Probably. What about you Jimmy?"

"Yeah. I'm feeling the need, you know? Tubes are calling, dude. Hard."

"Indeed," I said.

I looked at my partners and thought about all that we

had been through in the past few weeks. Or maybe months, who the hell really knew when it came to time anyway? So much had happened, it seemed like forever since Burroughs had first walked into my office so long ago.

Jimmy had taken a bad hit to his head on the coaster, and an even nastier fall, but nothing any worse than he hadn't already been exposed to by surfing into piers, jetties, or luxury yachts, all of which he had done on numerous occasions. If nothing else, the whole experience gave him a few more entries into his 'scar log'.

By the time I had gone down to the entrance of Space Mountain to get Simon and make it back with him to the floor level of the coaster room, Jimmy had been a little woozy but at least conscious and walking around, albeit in slow motion since he thought he had landed on Saturn and was space walking.

Zodar, however, had no prior experience surfing into inanimate objects himself, and as such, had suffered the hit and fall much harder. He had still been alive when we got to him, but that was about it.

Luckily, I knew just what to do with him. So we loaded him up onto a service truck (this took a while), drove him over to Animal Kingdom, and left him in the African wilderness.

The Disney staff found him early that morning and, thrilled at getting a free animal, especially a specimen of his size, nursed him back to health and had him out there thrilling the kids in no time, albeit under an extremely watchful eye and boatloads of heavy sedation.

I found it ironic that his well-being and care were now being provided by the very institution that he had been trying to overthrow. But I wax philosophic that way sometimes.

There was, of course, some controversy during his first few days there; some of those rather prissy tourist types (the kind that seem to know everything except the fact that nobody can stand them) questioned whether a moose was actually an animal indigenous to the African continent. But everyone generally ignored them and pretty soon the whole ruckus died down since the moose didn't really seem to mind being there and everyone thought he was a fine looking animal on the whole and so what if he wasn't from Africa anyway?

"So," I said, "you guys be needing a lift home?"

"That's okay," said Jimmy, "I'll just hitch a ride with Simon. Since he's heading that way anyway."

I looked at Simon with surprise.

"Yeah, well, I kind of bought a car the other day," he said.

"Really?"

"Yeah. '71 Caddy convertible."

"Sweet. Not quite an Impala, mind you, but sweet no less."

"I think so."

"Well, gentlemen," I said, "it's been quite the adventure. guess the only thing left is just to let you know how much I appreciate all of the help."

"Hey dude," Jimmy said, "No problem. And like, if anything gnarly comes up in the future, just let me know, okay?"

"Me too," Simon said. "This whole thing was a little weird, and I still have lots of problems with it, don't get me wrong, but it sure beats the hell out of my regular life.”

“Good to know,” I said. “I’ll make a point of it.

The three of us stood up and after exchanging a few brief “Goodbyes”, Jimmy and Simon headed out of the office. Just as he was about to shut the door, Simon paused and stuck his head back in.

“Say, Dick,” he said, “are you sure that Zodar is going to be okay in there? I mean, you don’t think he’s going to be able to escape or anything, do you?”

“We’re talking about Disney here. He’s worth too much to them. Between the staff and the meds? No. No way he gets out.”

“Yeah, I know. But still . . . I mean, he’s not in a *cage* or anything . . . and he’s not, you know, a regular moose. Are you *sure* he won’t be able to get out?”

“Simon, there’s a better chance of the Earth being attacked by a couple of teenage space aliens than there is of Zodar escaping. Okay?”

The concern melted from Simon’s face. “Yeah, you’re right. Well then, hey, take care, huh?”

“You too Simon,” I said. “And be sure to give my love to Pricilla.”

The door shut and I was left once again with just my thoughts. My calendar was empty for the foreseeable future, but after what I had just gone through, that was just as well. Both in mind and body, I felt I deserved a little R&R.

I lit a cigarette and smoked it in silence. Looked around my office and felt comfort in the familiar surroundings. Feeling a calm that I hadn’t felt in a long time, I turned to my potter’s wheel and flipped the switch for the motor. Once spinning, I wet my hands and gently

caressed the cool clay.
Soon I was fast asleep.

Epilogue

Berzdod and Xynelthorpe were up to no good again. The two young Barzanians from Sector BB34 had once again taken their father's Anti-Plasma Dissimilator without his permission, intent on ridding the galaxy of a few unnecessary stars. Dazed and confused, they bounded off drunkenly into the cosmos in the family Strato-glide, the Barzanian equivalent of a '72 Impala.

Several hours later they found themselves sitting next to the smoking hull of the Strato-glide, having crashed into a small white moon that Berzdod had mistaken for a small white hole. Although Berzdod frequently made this type of error, it really wasn't his fault this time, since Xynelthorpe, ever the prankster, had secretly replaced three of Berzdod's eyes with energy pellets.

Berzdod finished treating his radiation burns and looked up to see Xynelthorpe hopping about, still searching for his missing leg.

"Dad's gonna be pissed," Berzdod said.

"You're the idiot who keeps driving into planets," Xynelthorpe snorted.

Berzdod's scales bristled but he said nothing in his defense, knowing that if he did his brother would once again bring up the time he "winged" that Diridian space station, penetrating the hull and sending the whole outpost blowing about the galaxy like a balloon.

Fuming, he stood up, surveyed the surroundings stars, and tried to get a bearing on where they were. At that moment, however, one of the energy pellets in his eye cluster decided to spontaneously hyper-fuse, and the resulting jolt knocked him back to the ground.

Xynelthorpe snickered. "What a dork."

Really mad now, Berzdod stood up again and unstrapped the Anti-Plasma gun from his back. He sighted in on the yellow star to his right.

What the hell, he thought.

He shifted his footpods to plant himself better against the coming kick of the dissimilator and suddenly felt one of them slide away, causing him to stumble and inadvertently pull the trigger. On the ground once again, he looked with disgust to see what he'd tripped on and saw a small white orb covered with dimples and bearing strange markings that he didn't recognize; *Titleist*.

A crackling '*boom*' echoed back through the vacuum of space. Both Berzdod and Xynelthorpe looked up. The 90 megaton plasma orb had hit home alright, but not into the ugly yellow star. Instead, it had plowed neatly into a nearby blue and white planet.

"Nice shot, moron," Xynelthorpe noted.

220

www.ingramcontent.com/pod-product-compliance
Lightning Source LLC
Chambersburg PA
CBHW030643110726
47901CB00002B/554